LIKE THERE'S NO
TOMORROW

SANDRA HEILPERN

Cover design and typeset by Green Avenue Design.

Published by Cilento Publishing, Sydney Australia.

ISBN: 978-0-6482398-3-3

This novel is entirely a work of fiction. Any resemblance to actual persons, living or dead, is entirely coincidental.

"It is a curious situation that the sea, from which life first arose should now be threatened by the activities of one form of that life. But the sea, though changed in a sinister way, will continue to exist; the threat is rather to life itself."

Rachel Carson, The Sea Around Us July 1951

ONE

It is the first time they have been together for many years in this old house of hopes and disappointments, changing patterns of alliances and animosities. This house where each new baby wriggled to find its place in the pecking order, and each sibling rode the highs and lows of growing up, where open loving could never quite patch over the dark spaces.

Memories leach out from the walls and floral carpets, from the floppy lounge and kitchen table, as the four middle-aged siblings brush past each other, finding their new adult bearings.

They all feel the presence of their absent mother. She is impregnated in the very furnishings of this house. They expect to see her back when they walk into the kitchen. Her favourite cup lies within easy reach ready to be topped up from the china teapot in its woollen cosy.

They are tempted to think that she is just temporarily out of reach in her bedroom retreat, until the harsh reality hits. She has gone. Never coming back. Never feeling her touch. Never seeing her eyes light up. Never seeing the two of them together, him and her, with a love and understanding beyond their childrens' comprehension. And now the ghostly presence of their father. A hollow shell of himself. These adult children move around the empty spaces. Respectfully.

Cancer. They knew she had cancer. But somehow, they thought she would live forever.

❋ ❋ ❋

Carol's dream is shattered with her sharp ringtone. She struggles awake and reaches for her mobile. It is not quite six but already she can feel they are in for another scorcher. She mutters to herself that it's the fifth day over 40 degrees .

'Hi Dad..

'It's your mother,' he says. 'She died late last night.'

Carol gasps.

'The funeral is on Thursday. Can you come down and perhaps stay for a week? I'm asking all four of you to come as soon as possible.'

It is his tone more than anything that shocks her. So cold. So detached. So unreachable.

Questions that she can't ask him flood into her mind. When did the chemo stop working? Why didn't Dad let her know so she could come down earlier? How horrible was her death? Didn't her mother want her family around her?

'I'll get a flight and let you know when I'm arriving. I can catch a cab from the airport. Oh, Dad, I am so sorry.'

Carol stretches out, thankful for the fan that has been spinning above her all night and lets the sad realisation slowly enter her body. My mother is dead. She reaches out to the empty side of the bed, wishing there was still a 'him' who could hold her, who could share this sadness with her, who could lie there with her till her body succumbed to his touch and she let herself go into the world of loss.

Wide awake now, she sits up, reaches for the pad and pen next to her bed, and starts to jot down a to do list. Schedule her most urgent patients into the next two mornings. Cancel the rest of the bookings for the week. Contact Brenda who does physiotherapy locums. Book flight for tomorrow afternoon.

Under the shower, she lets the cold water run hard. She wonders how hot it has to be before the temperature melts the tarmac at the airport. When does bitumen go tacky? When does concrete expand and crack?

'Damn the heat wave,' she mutters. 'Damn the water restrictions and the two minute shower. Damn El Nino.'

As she pulls out a few clothes for her travel bag, she suddenly remembers funeral, good clothes, proper shoes. She reaches in for the little navy dress. Yes, it still fits. And the high sandals – she rubs the mould off with a bit of metho.

It is evening the next day when she flies out. She closes her eyes as soon as she buckles up, a sure discouragement to conversation from the woman next to her. She lets more of the true horror of her dad's phone call into her consciousness. She lets herself sink into the enormity of losing her mum. Yes, it's a big one.

Carol remembers the other big ones. Being left all those years ago with two young children was a big one. It is still raw, after all these years. Morning after morning, Leon, the father of their children would walk into the chaotic kitchen with a blissed-out, smug look on his face from his precisely twenty minutes' meditation in his perfect lotus position. Morning after morning as she juggled the porridge, the juice, the coffee and the burnt toast as well as the school lunches, and got herself ready for work, it slowly dawned on her that she did not want to keep living with all his rituals for peace and harmony, his wheat grass and bongs, their unfinished house with the dirt floor and half a bathroom. Gone was that pre-kids hot passion, the plans they used to make of building their house on the intentional community, each doing part-time work, and being self-sufficient while the world went mad.

Carol pulls herself up with a start. My mother is dead. She tries to grab it, hold it, feel it. But all she can do is recall that familiar gaping hole . Where was my mother for me when

I needed her most? Like when she phoned her mother to tell her that Leon had just pissed off with his young floozie to northern Queensland. What did her mother say? She was sure Carol could cope. No offer 'You must come down here.' No suggestion of 'Darling would you like me to come up?' Nothing.

Carol wonders to herself why she still goes there? Why she stills feel doubly abandoned, first by him and then by her? She's dead, you idiot. She's dead.

Another image floods in. Her very first memory.

It's Sunday morning, and all four of us kids are in the family room of our house, a large space for playing, cooking and eating around a big wooden table.

My sister Jennifer has toddler Andrew on her non-existent hip and is keeping him comforted and amused. My brother Robert is sitting at the table turning bits of plastic from a big box into machines whose wheels drive other bits of plastic round and round.

Sitting on the floor opposite the wooden flight of stairs that lead down from the bedrooms, I can feel the warmth of the wall against my back. I am sucking deeply on my thumb, and twirling my hair with the other hand. My eyes are fixed on the stairs.

At last, like every Sunday morning, my father bounces down the stairs. We all rush to greet him, except Robert who is engrossed with his lego. My father says, like he does every Sunday morning, 'My goodness, what good children you all are', and hugs us one by one. He sits me on the bench so that I can watch him get breakfast ready.

I breathe in the smells of pancakes and banana and honey.

When I look up towards the shut door of my parents' bedroom I sense the invisible sign that says 'Do not disturb'. I cannot remember ever having been inside that room.

Until I am old enough for sleepovers with my school friends, I think this is all perfectly normal.

The plane lands with a bump and taxies into the empty bay. Carol is not ready to face her father yet. So she passes on the taxi and settles on the long ride by train and bus. She needs a bit of extra time before she walks back through that door. She also needs time to adjust to the heavy Sydney air. She yearns desperately for rain and the sweet smell of eucalypt instead of the pungent smell of car exhaust.

She is the first to arrive.

Her dad gives her a big hug, suggests she might like to put her things in her old room and makes them both a cup of tea. He says they can talk together later once the others come as he couldn't bear to go through it all one by one. So they sit in silence on the verandah, looking out on the garden. He is in no state to be curious about what is happening for her, and she has no need to talk for talk's sake. She feels guilty about her recollections of her mother not being there for her. She tries to focus on all the times her mother was there for each of them. But looking back on it now, Carol knows that there was always a bit of her that was not there.

She sits next to her father and breathes deeply. The afternoon air, the air in this house and even on the verandah is heavy now with her mother's absence. Carol notices her father has slipped away. Back to his office, she guesses, she hopes.

On a whim, Carol lets herself be drawn up the stairs. She wills each step to be silent as she feels the old childhood apprehension in the back of her neck. She is sure the old rule of forbidden spaces still applies. She remembers the times she ran towards the door when she had scary dreams, turning at the last moment to Robert's room. He would always move over to make room for her and listen to her night-time fears and tell her that he would always be there.

Carol now stands in wonder at this perfectly normal looking bedroom. Normal queen-sized bed with bedside tables. Normal built-in wardrobes. Normal dressing table. What was she expecting? Chains hanging from the ceiling? Hand and foot cuffs on the non-existent bed posts? Puzzled she turns on her heel, heading for her old room, wondering how she can fill in the time till Jennifer arrives.

* * *

Andrew gets the same call soon after dinner. It is already dark in Washington State and the icy rain is beating loudly against the glass doors of the garden apartment.

'Hi Dad,' he says, turning up the volume, listening carefully to his father telling him in his so matter of fact voice, that his mother has died.

'So how soon can you get here?'

Andrew does a quick sum. 'Give me two days.'

Paul walks into the living room and sits down next to him, slumped over, head in his hands. Paul waits.

'I can't do it,' Andrew mutters. 'I can't make it in time for Mum's funeral. It's too far. I just can't do it.'

'Your mum?'

'Yes. That was Dad on the phone. It was weird. He said almost nothing except she had died and to come over straight away. He sounded so cold.'

'Oh that's terrible. I wonder why....'

'Oh, we knew she was sick. But not that sick.'

'Andrew, you do need to go. Afterwards, you know, you would never ...'

'Yeah. I need to go.'

'We can do it,' Paul said.

They sit in silence for a while, Paul cradling Andrew, and Andrew going limp, feeling safe in his lover's arms.

Eventually Paul says, 'I'll get you a flight for early tomorrow morning. And I'll phone the school. You need two weeks off? OK?'

'OK.'

Paul goes to their bedroom and comes back laden with Andrew's coat, scarf, swimmers, goggles and a towel.

'Now, go do laps.'

'Fuck, what would I do without you?'

Andrew obeys. He drives the short distance to the indoor pool, peels off his winter layers, changes into his swimmers and lowers himself into the warm water, wetting his goggles and placing them on this face. He pushes off, entering the meditative world of laps. Don't count them. Don't think. Just breathe. His long arms and legs in automatic. Head turning, breathing. In for one, slowly bubble out two three four. Expand rib cage for one, stretch out the fingers, kick one two three four. The voice of his old coach is still in his head as he transforms into a mindless, graceful sea creature, gliding, breathing, tumble turning, up and down. Forty minutes and he is done. He dries off, changes and returns home, calmer now, not a trace of the old asthma.

A ticket waits for him, on the bed, next to his travelling bag.

'Oh, Paul, I can't afford a seat up the front.'

'I can. It's not very often your mother dies.'

'No. No it's not. Thank you. I'll do the same for you one day.'

Andrew rifles through his wardrobe searching for clothes for the unseasonably warm autumn back home, still struggling with Paul's generosity. Still wanting to do it all, all by himself.

✳ ✳ ✳

Jennifer's mobile wakes her. She sits up straight and wonders what she was doing, sleeping in the barn. Then the horror of the night before starts to replay in her head.

She gropes for the ringing mobile in the dim light.

'Hi Dad.'

She listens carefully as he repeats his story.

'Jennifer, are you still there?'

'Yes. I'm here Dad. I can't talk just now. But I'll be there. I'll get a flight. I'll be there.'

Jennifer lies motionless as the drama of the early morning replays in her head. She remembers it started just before morning light when she was aware that John was awake, as he was most mornings now, waiting for the first sun to appear at their eastern window.

They both heard the dog barking furiously.

She watched as John rubbed his eyes and let his hands wander over his forehead, across the top of his big boney head and down to the back of his neck, where he tried in vain, as he did each morning, to ease the tight muscles.

He muttered his usual early morning mantra, 'Bloody drought. Bloody dog,' as he stumbled into the big farm kitchen. Soon he was shouting, 'Jen, get up! Get your gear on, something's up. Grab your phone.'

Jennifer came down as he was washing blood off the kelpie's legs checking to see where she was injured.

'Not her blood,' he said as he grabbed his jacket from the hook by the door and raced across to the bike shed, whistling for the kelpie to follow.

Jennifer just had time to zip up her jacket as she jumped onto the back of the motor bike. He shouted, 'GO', to the dog, and they followed her as she led them to the horse paddock.

In the early morning light Jennifer could make out the shape of the new mare, Bonnie, lying in a pool of blood. John shouted 'Out of there, you mongrel', to the dog, who had entered the dark sticky mess, facing John, head up, waiting for 'Good dog'. John raced towards the horse, feeling her neck for a pulse. 'Dammit, so where's the bloody foal?'

Looking around they spot her, among the cluster of the other horses, teetering on her long baby legs, half hidden in the shadows.

Jennifer walked slowly towards her, whispering shush shush sounds, stretching out her hand. John crept up behind her and handed her a looped rope.

'Walk her home, Jen. I'll stay here a while.'

Soon after she heard the shot ring out.

Now Jennifer wide awake, reaches out and pats the sleeping foal. Midday already. But she is in no way ready to face John and his seething anger. Like everything else, he'll be blaming the mare's haemorrhage on the drought.

Just a few more minutes. She turns to the foal. Both our mothers are gone. The reality of her father's phone call begins to bear down on her. Her mother dead? Not sick. Not dying. Dead. She does not want to face her siblings or her father. Come on Jennifer, she tells herself. Just go.

She books the last ticket on the early flight next morning. She calls the hospital. She packs. John phones to let her know he has gone to town for some supplies and will be home late. He hangs up before she can tell him about her mother. She writes him a note and sticks it on the fridge adding clear instructions about the foal. Two more feeds and her own simple dinner. Six formula bottles stacked in front of the beer in the fridge. She doesn't care that there is hardly any food there. She sets her alarm for 5 am, and heads for her daughter's empty bed, luggage within reach.

* * *

Robert gets the call later that same morning. He is relieved his dad knows not to call too early because he is best left alone before ten or eleven. He listens carefully to every word. Questions. He starts to ask, how come ….?

But his father cuts him off. 'We can talk when you come down.'

'I'll be there. Don't worry, Dad. I will.'

Robert hears the click and finishes, 'I will. I promise, I will.'

He curls up on his side, and despite the heat of the day, pulls the light blanket over himself. He feels the sadness creeping up into his body as he gives way. He is no stranger to sobbing. At least, he tells himself, today I have a good reason.

The day is almost over before he is up, showered, dressed, fed, medicated and ready for the work he needs to do in the shed.

'Sorry, mate,' he says to the old ute that is still up on blocks, waiting for him to get around to fixing its electrics.

He turns his attention to the motor bike, knowing that it only needs a few tweaks and adjustments to get it in working order.

'You,' he says, 'will just have to do. Bit much eh, for a long ride to Sydney on a 120cc but you and me, we can do it.'

He likes riding through the night. Cooler in his leathers. Taking the quiet roads, the back roads, avoiding the B-double and B-triple trucks.

He packs the side panniers with clothes and carefully adds his medication to his toilet bag. He finishes off the bowl of left-over stir-fry in the fridge, grabs his wallet, keys and mobile, closes all the doors and windows and draws the curtains against the heat of the days. Before he puts on his helmet he sits astride the bike, slowly calming his breath, willing his trembling right leg to settle down, focusing his mind on the eagle tattoo on the inside of his left elbow, he pauses, waiting for its noble strength to start beating through his body.

TWO

Carol and Jennifer, feeling like strangers in the house they grew up in, and feeling like strangers with each other, flop down in the sticky heat, moving their chairs to catch the slight easterly breeze on the big verandah.

Long, is how Carol remembers Jennifer as she glances over to her sister. She was always long, with long skinny legs, long arms that could reach very high places, long hair always back. But today, she just looks stretched by some unseen tension, pulling her body every which way.

Jennifer, her mind barely able to leave the foal in the hay-shed, is worried that John will be too preoccupied with his own problems to give it its bottle. She reaches for her phone and sends him another message.

Carol notices that Jen's pale nondescript hair has escaped the eternal pony tail. She sees the criss-cross lines around Jen's mouth, and the long fingers with a life of their own, twitching slightly in her lap. Even those intense blue eyes have no sparkle today.

In between the silences, Carol tries to make conversation. Questions about how's John, how are you making out in the drought, how are the twins, are they still at boarding school, how's your job at the hospital, how's your singing group going? They fall barely answered and lie in a little heap on the floor between them.

Instead she answers the questions that Jennifer hasn't asked, and talks out loud about her own physiotherapy practice, how Jonah and Brook are getting on now that they have both left home, how strange it is after all this time to have just herself to look after, and how, no, she still doesn't have a special man in her life, but not for lack of wanting it. Well, wanting it some of the time.

It is a welcome relief when their father appears, saying that it's time for the evening news, and that Thai take-away has been delivered. They eat mechanically watching the dramas of the day randomly unfold, the war wherever, the same looking civilians in the same living hell, the long crack in the Antarctic ice, the methane escaping and burning in Siberia, a truck over-turning on the Pacific Highway and a gangland shooting on someone's front lawn. Following their father's suggestion the sisters climb the stairs to their old bedrooms, Jennifer tapping a message to John as she climbs the stairs. Carol smiles at the familiar wood panelling and feels the slide of her hand on the smooth wooden hand-rail. She wonders that this house still looks the same since they all left home. A solid little brick bungalow, with a second floor of bedrooms added as the family swelled from two to six.

Carol walks past the main bedroom and thinks of her father, wondering how he can do that, sleep in the same bed as he shared with her all those years. It gives her the creeps just to know he is there and that her mother is not.

She takes a sleeping pill hoping to crash out till morning.

Robert cuts the motor bike and pushes it effortlessly down the driveway. His fingers find the hidden front door key and he lets himself into the house. He rattles around in the kitchen finding left-overs, washes them down with a cold beer and makes his way up to his old bedroom across the hall on the boys' side of the house.

✳ ✳ ✳

Andrew arrives early the next morning. Robert, the only one up, answers the door bell. He gives Andrew a big hug and looks searchingly at his face to check he is OK. Andrew is not OK. He is somewhat peeved that no-one bothered to come to the airport. Surely they would know he has been travelling forever, changing planes and hanging around transit lounges. Robert tries appeasement. Have a shower mate. Get changed. What would you like for breakfast? Andrew falls for the old charm. Thanks. Yeah a shower would be good. Any chance of some eggs and bacon?

THREE

Breakfast. They take their old seats around the kitchen table leaving the chair at the head empty for their father. Andrew removes the empty chair at the other end of the table, looking for a space to put it, and finally takes it out the back door into the garden. Their dad arrives and takes his place. The funeral. He needs to tell them the arrangements he has already made for later that day. He says he doesn't think he will be able to say anything. He looks around expectantly for offers. Andrew says he would like to prepare a play list of her favourite music. Blues. Jennifer shakes her head. Robert says he would like to say something. Carol says that if her father could write out what he wants to say, then she could read it out. 'No, just the one from Robert will be enough,' he says.

'Something else,' he says. 'You must be wondering why I asked you to stay longer.'

He tells them he is putting the house on the market and moving down to the holiday shack, on the south coast. He wants it all cleared out. The basement, the bedrooms, the lot. He puts his hands down flat on the table, eases himself out of the chair, and shambles out of the room.

Their eyes follow him. Their father has shrunk into an old man.

Carol breaks the silence.

'Well now it's pretty clear why he wants us to stay on. But I can't help thinking he isn't saying that he needs us here, for him, now that he is all alone.'

'He hasn't mentioned her once.' Jennifer's face crumples as she speaks. 'Not her cancer, not how she died. Not why they didn't tell us.'

'Give him time, Jen.' Robert moves his chair a bit closer to her. 'He's not up to talking much at all.'

'I need to start on that music,' Andrew says, scraping back his chair.

'And I guess I need to start writing something. Hey guys, give me a hand here. What do you reckon? What would she have wanted us to say about her?'

Jennifer gets a pad and pen.

'We only have a few hours,' she says. 'We'd better get down to it now.'

'I want you two to know,' Robert says looking at each of his sisters in turn. 'I'm travelling OK at the moment. I take my meds.'

Carol glances across to Robert, pleased to see that he is coping. She still hangs onto the image of the old Robert, the well Robert, his athlete's body and healthy glow. But now she can see he has aged so much more than the rest of them, even Jennifer. Hair loss, a suggestion of a stoop and hollow chest, the slight tremor in his leg he ignores, his slower careful pace. She feels a stab of guilt about losing contact with him, conveniently dismissing him and his psychosis all these years. She feels guilty that she left home to start her own life, leaving Robert for her parents to deal with as best they could.

But then, she thinks, she wasn't the only one. Big sister Jennifer heading off to do nursing, and then falling in love with the motor bike accident multiple fractures farmer from way out west, and Andrew, the youngest of them heading off to the USA as soon as he got his music degree. One way or another they all fled.

'So Carol, what do you remember about her?' Jennifer is asking. Robert is sitting with pen poised.

'Sorry, what have you got so far?'

* * *

Their mother's final send off is another cremation on a busy day at the cold and impersonal building. It stands in the shadow of its tall chimney, surrounded by urban bushland. In the late afternoon heat they come, neighbours, her old friends, his business contacts and their wives. They park their air-conditioned cars, search for the right hall, amble in to haunting blues, and sit in respectful silence, waiting. Robert walks out front to the podium, standing in front of the small coffin. He looks around the hall, half filled with people he hardly knows, and starts reading.

'Our mother, your friend, Gabrielle O'Brien, was a very special person …'

Jennifer, Carol and Andrew sit straight, in the front row, with their father. They hear the words in Robert's beautiful voice. Strong today. Passionate and loving. They hear how she had been a very special mother to each of them, how she and their dad had a loving bond that carried them through the good times and the not so good, how they had waited for ten years before having children so that they could provide for all their needs, how she had waited till they had all left home before she took up her own studies and a new career. He tells silly anecdotes. He makes them laugh and he makes them cry.

They watch as the coffin slides behind the curtain to the incinerator. They move out into the rose garden for wine and coffee, sandwiches and scones. They make small talk to strangers who knew their mother.

Nobody mentions the absence of any other relatives. Nobody mentions that the seriousness of her illness was kept secret even from her children.

Finally, it is over. The staff is hovering to make rose garden ready for the next lot of mourners. They are free to go home.

✳ ✳ ✳

That night they sit around after another takeaway Thai, each reluctant to retreat into the loneliness of their bedrooms. Their father disappears into his study. They move into the family lounge room, Carol and Jennifer at each end of the floppy three seater lounge, Andrew and Robert circling around before flopping down in the two armchairs.

Carol breaks the silence. 'Let's not turn on the TV. I don't think I could stand it tonight'.

No one disagrees.

Andrew and Robert turn their chairs away from the TV so that they are all facing each other, avoiding contact, searching the walls with the pastoral oil paintings, the faintly striped long curtains, bracket lighting in the shape of candle flames, and the one feature wall painted in a deep blue grey. Each of them fragmented from the day's event, each of them yearning for human comfort that none of them is able to give.

'So', Carol suggests, 'how would it be if we talked a bit about us?'

'Let's go in reverse order,' she says. 'Andrew, could you start?

He stares blankly at her.

'So,' she prompts, 'what is the most important thing about your life at the moment?'

Andrew shuffles in the arm chair. Recrosses his long legs. He and Jennifer. Both long. Both with their mother's intense blue eyes. Both so Nordic. Andrew sits there thinking. His tapered fingers touching.

He smiles. 'Love. Love is the most important thing in my life now. Paul and I. And me and Christopher.'

He goes on.

'It feels good.' The words start tumbling out.

Meeting Paul in a gay bar. Instant magic between them. A crazy debauched romance. Andrew still married to Lisa. Christopher just a toddler. And Paul, pushing away his pain of the early HIV days, now in a middle-age frenzy of partying, snorting, spending, indulging, and then finding Andrew looking lost in a gay bar and leading him slowly into the other world of gay love, gay sex, gay partying.

Andrew tells them very little of his marriage crashing out of control but he does tell them that he knew he couldn't keep up this life with Paul and still be a part-time father to Christopher. So he'd told Paul that things had to be different.

'I'd told him that he is just a little kid and that we need to be organised, disciplined, safe, like a proper family.'

And to his surprise Paul had said, 'Yeah, why not?'

'So,' Andrew tells them, 'it's working, with me and Paul. He adores Christopher. They go tramping off in the mountains doing north American hero stuff that I am hopeless at. But mostly there is lots of love in our house. And,' he smiles, 'no secrets.'

'Have you ever thought about coming back here?' Robert asks.

'No. And I have the perfect excuse. I could never take Christopher away from Lisa, and I could never leave him there.'

'How about your music?' Jennifer wonders out loud.

'I finally gave up on being famous,' he says. 'Teaching school kids is fine most of the time. Every now and then I get one that has real talent, and it's pretty special to be able to see that and nurture and encourage it. Teaching gives me more Christopher time too, and that works for all of us.'

Carol suddenly realises they are all looking at her. Yes, next youngest. Her turn.

She is surprised at what pops out of her mouth. She tells them that her life has become, if anything, too easy, after all that chaos of bringing up two kids as a single mum and starting her own therapy practice. She tells them about worrying that Jonah was too good, and that Brook was always getting into trouble. But now they had both left home. Home was the big constant in her life. Home was where she could be herself, play her own music, paint the walls with yellows and golds, plant out a garden that brought the birds. What could possibly be wrong with a little wooden house on the coast, in the most iconic beach town in all of NSW?'

'Except,' she adds quietly, 'sometimes…sometimes, I wish it wasn't just me.'

They wait. She doesn't go on.

'How about all that protesting you used to do, up there in the forest?' asks Robert. 'I was so proud of my little eco-terrorist sister, getting stoned and locking onto bulldozers to stop the loggers.'

And suddenly she finds herself telling them what she hasn't quite managed to tell herself. How activism had gone onto the back burner. How people weren't protesting anymore. How it was like, social media had taken over, and if you hit the sign button for a different campaign every week, then that counted. Well they all knew it didn't count much at all. But they had given up on protests. The politicians didn't take notice of protests anymore. Did they? They only took notice of the polls.'

Carol trails off with, 'It sounds a bit feeble doesn't it? Life's got too easy.'

'Don't you care anymore?' Robert again, leaning forward, pressing her buttons, wanting some response, any response, as long as it's real.

'Of course I care. I care hugely about the mess we are leaving our kids and especially our unborn grandkids. I care hugely about the two big ones of too many of us on this planet and too much carbon dioxide and methane we are mindlessly releasing. I can see climate change creeping up on us, while all our politicians care about is getting back in for another term.'

Tears of frustration start running down her face.

'But I don't know what to do about it anymore. We used to know what to do. And we used to feel good about doing it. Saving a compartment of old growth forest was really something. But it's all so fucking useless now. It's got so much bigger than a bit of forest. And besides, nobody listens!'

And to her own horror, she puts her head into her hands and sobs. 'I so wanted to be with her once more before she died.'

Jennifer moves across to sit close to Carol on the lounge. She wraps her long arms around her, and strokes her gently.

Andrew and Robert sit quietly. Then Robert gets up and comes back with a box of tissues. Andrew gets up and comes back with four cold beers.

Carol struggles free and shrugs. 'Sorry.' Mops up and grabs a beer. Jennifer straightens up. Reaches for her phone. Does a quick text.

'Thanks guys,' as she also takes a beer.

All eyes are on Robert.

'I'm turning 50 this year,' Robert begins, 'and the stats on schizophrenia tell us that if I haven't killed myself by now, then life will start getting less crazy, less intense and less out of control. The stats also tell me that I should be less healthy for my age, more likely to have diabetes, kidney failure and heart trouble, let alone the odd cancer, but so far none of these have happened.'

He pauses.

'But I guess that's not really answering the question - what is the most important thing in my life at the moment.'

'When I got sick, like at first, it was as if a huge tragedy came crashing down on this whole family. Let's face it. I was really smart. I was a big sporting hero. I was heading for a great life, and everyone was so proud of me. Then boff. All gone. No more.'

Robert starts walking slowly up and down.

'So, what's good about now is that the only expectation anyone has of me anymore is that I take my meds and I manage that, well, most of the time. So in a way I am free from any expectations. I don't even have expectations of myself. Most days my world stops at the front gate. Inside that, is my garden. It gets most of my attention and the house virtually none of it. I play it all out there. Killing is for weeds. Nurturing is for seedlings. It's a whole lot easier than doing people.'

'And what else Robert? What else do you do?' Andrew wants to know.

'I splurge as much as you can on a part pension, in town, at the motor bike club. I even coach some of their kids in soccer. I listen to a bit of pub music.'

Robert sits back down.

'Oh, and I do a bit of writing on the computer. You know, stories and stuff.'

Carol asks, 'Really when did you start that?'

'In prison. Doing a journal. Then I got onto stories.'

None of them go there, with prison. But Carol gets flashes of when her friends did time for drugs when they were all so much younger. She thinks of visiting the old Grafton jail in the middle of winter, the long wait through security, sitting with them in their white overalls with the zip up the back, them looking pale and so vulnerable, a pile of coins for the Coke machine, trying to make small talk so as to avoid the big talk of what it was really like in there. She jolts herself back to the present.

'That's great, Robert,' she manages, 'I've always wanted to do some writing myself.'

All eyes turn to Jennifer.

'I guess it's my turn. I don't know where to start.'

Andrew asks, 'What's with all this texting? You can hardly leave your phone alone. What's going on?'

'There's a newborn foal in the hay-shed, and I'm worried that John will forget to give it is bottle.'

'You're worried about a foal? I thought there was the mother of all droughts going on.'

Andrew's directness throws Jennifer. The drought has become so much part of her very being that she hardly thinks of it as a separate thing anymore.

'You want to know about the drought? I'll tell you about the drought then.'

Jennifer draws breath, and then lets fly like it was all their fault about the drought, like it was time they stopped thinking about their trivial love life, and their trivial loss of protests, and their trivial garden, for fuck's sake, and started hearing what a real-life drought was like.

'The farm's given us no real income for three years, other than selling off our breeding stock for a pittance. We've long gone through our savings, and are living off loans from a bank that won't give us loans anymore and wants to put our farm on the market, except no-one would be stupid enough to buy it. The boarding school is threatening to send the kids home because we owe fees and John's parents say they can't pay them any longer. The suicide rate at home has skyrocketed and the hospital where I work knocks back mental health patients who have nowhere else to go. And John keeps selling off stuff for seeds to plant although the soil is dead dry and no rain is forecast for the rest of this autumn. What else do you want to know?'

'Oh, Jennifer, I am so sorry.' Carol wants to physically reach out to her sister. But she can't. Jennifer is too distant from her, untouchable in her world of drought and despair.

'Me too.' Andrew is shocked at the shallow fortune of his life. He leans towards Jennifer and asks, 'How do you and John cope with all that? Do you have any help?'

'We don't cope. John is a mess. He doesn't do help.'

Robert sighs. He knows drought. He knows the drought of empty feelings. After tidal waves of fear and anger. He knows drought in his body when his skin goes dry and his hair lifeless. He knows drought when the money runs out. He knows the desperate longing for water to make his life bloom. He sits with it.

They all feel helpless about the drought. They feel helpless about Jennifer. Old stuff. They don't know how to show her support. They never have. It always flowed the other way.

They start standing up, stretching, taking their empty cans to the kitchen and making their way up the stairs. Carol hears Andrew say to Robert, 'Perhaps we'll start watching TV again tomorrow night.'

Over the next few days they pick up the old threads. Old alliances re-form. Jennifer and Andrew, the oldest and the youngest, sit talking together on the window seat for hours, just like they used to. The bookends.

'They are still so gorgeous,' Carol says to herself. She can't help comparing them to Robert and herself. Both chunkier, clunkier. Their dad's broad shoulders and tough-looking calf muscles that keep them firmly in contact with the earth. The blond hair turning to brown as they grew older. They wear their father's worry lines on their foreheads. Hers hidden by a fringe. His bare.

Robert and Carol, never ones for sitting, shuffle about almost dragging their big toes along the carpet like they used to, driving their mother demented with 'I'm bored, Mum.'

Suddenly they remember the garden. They raid the tool shed. Together they prune the roses, cut back the hydrangeas, saw the dead wood off the fruit trees. No tree or shrub in that old garden escapes their manic energy as they lay bare to each other failed relationships, drugs and their shared guilt of abandoning their parents and each other.

They vow to do better with Dad from now on and to stay in touch with each other. Carol can tell that Robert is far from the old Robert she knew. Give-away signs. Close up she can see his hair has baldish patches. He carries his once beautifully athletic body like a burden he has to lug around. He's locked away inside himself. Sometimes, the old Robert pops out for a few moments, in a throw away line with a twinkle in his eyes, in a single graceful beautiful movement reminiscent of his old self.

By the third day it is time to start on the basement.

Carol starts pulling away from her siblings. Watching. Watching them pulling out boxes. 'Oos' and 'Ahhs' at forgotten treasures. Photos, soccer medals, school badges and magazines. Clothes from long forgotten teenage fashions. Hockey sticks, footballs, the doll's house.

From the sidelines she watches them dispatch items to the three growing piles - 'throw out' 'charity bin' and 'keep'.

'C'mon Carol, give us a hand. Where's your 'keep' pile?'

Carol starts tossing the remnants of her childhood and adolescence anywhere but 'keep'. She has no 'keep' pile but she keeps filling the big green plastic bags for 'throw out' and 'charity bin' and dragging them up to the top of the driveway.

Tipping out the contents of an old duffel bag Carol's fingers wrap around a small folder that looks strangely important. Then she remembers. It's a chart and a tape from an old astrological consultation. She puts it aside and later slides it into her day-pack for safe keeping.

At their dad's insistence they start on 'Mother's things'. For him it had always been Mother's dinner sets, Mother's table linen and Mother's everything else.

Carol watches detachedly as Robert lets Jennifer have first choice and then silently puts aside whatever she rejects. Jennifer is in charge. Robert compliant. Another old pattern playing out.

Andrew catches Carol's eye. She nods. They slip out, race upstairs, go to their rooms, and then slip out the back door in swimmers and t-shirts, hats and thongs, their towels slung over their shoulders. They make it to the corner of the street before bursting out laughing.

'I.. I.. I..' Andrew is gasping for breath, 'couldn't stand it any longer.'

'Me neither.'

They walk quickly down the hill to the bay, their feet taking them through the old familiar short cut through lanes and small parklands.

They are mindlessly kicking the dead leaves that have formed in piles under the huge camphor laurel trees.

Andrew stops. 'What's going on? Camphors don't drop their leaves.'

Carol gazes up at the once beautiful canopy. 'It's the drought. They do this up north when we have big El Ninos. It's a survival thing. They are cutting down their evaporation.'

'But here?'

'I've never heard of it happening this far south.'

Silent now, slower now, they walk the rest of the way, down to the bay.

Andrew throws his things on the sand, peels off his t-shirt, and races into the water. Soon he is in rhythm, long arms propelling him, feet kicking white water, heading north across the wide expanse of Balmoral Beach.

Carol watches, takes her time to pile her things next to Andrew's on the sand. She wanders down to the water slowly walking deeper and deeper, marvelling that the water is still warm and that the cold autumn currents have not kicked in. She floats on her back and pictures Robert and Jennifer in the basement, slowly picking over their mother's possessions. She wonders about those two. Collectors. And thinks of how she has been downsizing ever since Jonah and Brook left home. She wonders for a moment if there might have been something her kids would have liked from the grandmother they hardly knew. Something of family heritage. And then, a quick dismissal. They have their own heritage. Brook with the age-old methods of biodynamic farming and Jonah with his tireless protests for the ancient native forests.

Refreshed and feeling guilty, Carol and Andrew make their way slowly back up to the house. Andrew breaks the silence.

'You mightn't remember, those nights when I got asthma.'

'No, I don't remember much about that,' Carol admits.

'She used to prop me up with pillows and sit on my bed. And she would make me look at her. And then she would tell me to breathe with her. And we would breathe in together and slowly all the way out, usually with me coughing, and we would just sit there, opposite each other, and even though I was scared shitless, I knew that if she stayed there, and if I followed her breath, I would make it till morning, and then it would be OK.'

'And in the morning,' he goes on, 'she would slip out once I'd fallen asleep and later Dad would pop his head around.

'Feeling better now, son?' he would ask, and I would have to say yeah, because he couldn't stand it when I'd tell him that I couldn't breathe last night and it was really scary.'

'What was it about Dad,' Andrew goes on, 'that everything had to be OK.'

'I remember there were some mornings when Dad would say that we had to be good kids because Mum was still asleep and you'd been sick with asthma, but were feeling better now.'

'Mum often said we had to be good kids for Dad too. Do you remember when it was time for him to come home from work, and she would say he would be tired after a busy day and we weren't to fight when he got home?'

'I think you remember a lot more than I do about when we were kids, Andrew.'

'Yeah. Sometimes I wish I didn't.'

Once home, they slip inside, quickly shower and change and join Jennifer and Robert having cold beers in the kitchen.

Silence.

Their dad joins them.

'Well done. You boys can take the car and drop off the bags at St Vinnies. I've phoned the Council for a special pick up for the rest.'

He takes a beer and they all stand around in silence.

Finally he says to Carol, 'We can take your mother's car. You can drive if you like. I want to try that new Greek place. They do take-aways now. Any special requests for dinner?'

'Whatever.'

'You choose.'

Jennifer starts tidying up the kitchen as they all leave.

Carol can't believe her mother's old Toyota still works. Must be thirty years old. A survivor of all the bumps and clutch damage of four teenagers learning to drive. As she carefully reverses it out of the driveway her heart sinks at the lack of power steering. How did we do it?

They drive to the shops in silence. She parks. Her father heaves himself out of the sunken seat.

'Take your time, Dad. I'll enjoy some quiet time to myself.' As she feels around her day-pack for a tissue her hand comes across the astrology tape she had rescued that day. She smiles as she remembers her ex had given her a present of the consultation for her twenty-eighth birthday. That was just before he left her and the kids for his latest baby-faced lover. Carol puts the tape in the old Toyota's tape deck, and gazes in amazement as the little wheels start moving. She soon realises that it is playing towards the end of the consultation. She sighs as she sits back and shuts her eyes to listen to the astrologer's soft, kind voice.

'Look, Carol,' he is saying, 'I can tell that things are pretty rough for you at the moment and there will be big changes in your life in the next few months that are going to be even harder.'

'Big changes?' She hears her own young innocent voice ask. 'Like what?'

'I'm not a clairvoyant, Carol. I can't read the future. But I can see the patterns, the highs and lows, the times that really challenge you and the strengths you can call on to meet these challenges.'

There was a long pause. She could hear him let out a sigh.

'When things get tough for you, and for many of us, we are tempted to hang onto what we have, because the thing we fear most is letting go. Know that fear of letting go. Let it in. Experience it. Just know it.'

Another sigh. She remembers his frustration that she didn't ask any questions.

'It must seem a long way off for you, but when you are about ….' and Carol could hear the rustle of papers, 'ah yes, about forty-two, you will have the chance to let go of a lot of what you want to hang onto. Letting go is the first step to letting go fear of death. You can then truly live for the moment. You can take more control of your own life instead of letting your fears take control of you.'

She can hear his chair scrape as he stood up and then her chair scrape too.

'You have great inner strength, Carol. Hard lessons, yes, but you have love from many people in your life and you have determination and that is a very big plus.'

Click. Silence. She ejects and puts the tape back into her bag.

Her Dad opens the passenger door of the old Toyota carefully balancing plastic bags full of stacked plastic boxes that smell delicious. Suddenly Carol realises that she is starving. In her head she starts forming a conversation she knows she will have to have with her father very soon. But not now. It will have to wait.

❋ ❋ ❋

The Greek take-away is finished, Andrew and Robert head for the living room, searching for a TV program or a movie.

Jennifer and Carol clear away the dinner remains and wander in a short time later.

'Hey, turn that thing off,' Jennifer says, pulling an old envelope out of her jeans pocket.

'I found this today, in the table linen. I want to read it to you. It's a story apparently our mum wrote for a competition. There's a rejection slip in there saying the topic was too confronting for the readers of The Australian Women's Weekly. It's dated, well, a year before I was born. So she was married. I want to read it out to you?'

'Yes.'

'Yes.'

'Go ahead.'

ICE by Gabrielle Anne Parker

I often noticed my mother looking at us. First at my older sister, and then at me. Her glance would go from one to the other, sweeping backwards and forwards looking slightly puzzled.

By the time my older sister was eleven she had tits and periods. By the time I was fourteen I had neither. My sister was round and pretty, pale and cautious. I had a sunbaked skinny little body. And I had no fear. I loved speeding down the big hills on my Malvern Star two-wheeler with the wind rushing past my face. I loved summer days at the beach, in my blue speedo with outsized green rubber flippers on my feet, stroking out to catch the huge Christmas waves at Bondi, riding in on top of the world and then crashing down into a sea of white foam not knowing or caring which way was up.

I used to look at her, my older sister, with a detached curiosity. Her tits fascinated me. Her roundness. Her full stomach. Her thighs. The strange sweet sour smell that would linger in her bed clothes and pyjamas. The times when she was too cranky to play and then the week of the thin elastic belt around her waist, with the pins at the ends of the flaps, holding her pad in place between her legs.

At fourteen my body was still ten years old. Each day I would look at it in the bathroom mirror and see a flat chest, flat stomach, flat legs. I started looking at our female relatives, women on the bus, women in shops, women at the beach, and I could find none without breasts, none with chests as flat as mine. I used to wonder when it would change and why not now.

At school, we never talked about getting our first bra. But we all knew when another girl slipped through to womanhood. We knew from the rituals of the gym changing room, from the row of girls who faced their lockers, with pink or white straps across their backs and thinner straps over their shoulders.

We who faced anywhere had no straps. We scrunched our uniforms into our lockers and raced out eager to be first on the gym equipment.

All that school year the row of backs with their pink and white straps got longer and longer. Suddenly there was only me and Penelope and Charlotte left, and then only me and Charlotte, and then only me.

I didn't do gym for a while. I sprained my ankle, and it wouldn't heal properly. I had a cold with a lingering cough which got much worse with exercise. I had a stomach ache on Tuesdays.

But I still managed to go ice skating.

'Please Mum, I have to practice my eights, and my spins.'

And Mum who wanted so very dearly to have graceful and accomplished girls would say, 'Alright dear. But be home before dark.'

And so every afternoon that winter I walked past the usual crowd waiting for the school special, and set off over the tramlines, under the row of big Moreton Bay fig trees, across the expanse of grass to the Ice Palais.

As soon as I walk in I can hear the music playing the skater's waltz. I can feel the chill hit my face. I pull from my globite suitcase, my white skates, my thick socks, my button hook to pull the laces tight, and my short blue velvet dress with the twirly skirt and the pale blue pants to match. In minutes I am on the ice. A few rounds and then into the middle of the rink and I quicken the pace. I do a 'three' and skate backwards on one foot, one skate crosses over the other, I reach my arms far out to one side, curve my body and bend my knees and then suddenly I am spinning, faster and faster, my arms stretched way out to the sides and then crossed over in front to finish off. Then again I go faster and faster, and I do a jump and land, yes, on one leg, breathtakingly close to a wobbly beginner. I show off shamelessly. I weigh nothing at all. I can leap in the air. I can spin until I am beyond dizziness. I can weave in and out of the other skaters.

And then I do what she would never approve of. I go in the races. I stand with my age group. My head is level with their shoulders. Mostly boys. No handicaps here. And we're off. I love it. I push my legs until the front of my boots press hard into my shin bones. I round my shoulders and lean forward, arms swinging, fingers just above the ice. I do cross steps as I go round the curves. I weave and duck and wriggle my way to the inside of the circle, where it's faster, tighter, a maze of arms and shoulders swinging in my face, across my legs, in front of my body. They say I show promise. I promise myself that I will never never tell my mother.

I skate till the very last minute of the session. I never have time to change. I stuff my school uniform and my skates into my school case, change back into my school shoes and socks, run for the 5.30 bus in my little blue velvet dress.

This bus is always crowded. It's full of people going home from work. There are young bank clerks in grey suits and shop assistants in black dresses. There are older men upstairs with Daily Mirrors, reading the sports sections and smoking Craven A's. I am a child. I have to stand downstairs. I have to stretch up to hold onto the leather strap hanging from the chrome bar which runs down the middle of the bus. I lurch with the movement of the bus, my case between my feet.

But my head is still in the Ice Palais. I am racing like never before. I am way out in front. This skinny little kid, breaking away from the pack, and all the clapping and the cheering is for me. The afternoon crowd at the Ice Palais is going mad.

It's my stop. I jump off the bus. I run down the hill. I turn into our driveway, run up the side passage, and rush in the back door. It slams shut as I shout to my mother who is three paces from me in the kitchen, 'It's me, Mum. I'm home!'

I bend over to pick up Pudding, our ginger cat who has sat himself on my feet. And as I get my hands under his big fat fluffy body I hear the gasp behind me as my mother's breath is being sucked in.

'It's come,' she says out loud. 'O Lord, it has finally come!'

She places her hands on my shoulders and gently turns me around to face her. She caresses my face with her hands. She kisses me. She pulls me towards her and wraps me in her arms. I feel so safe. I look at her face and see tears running down her cheeks.

Finally, she says. 'Come I'll run you a bath.' I have never seen my mother cry before or since. I have never felt her hands cupping my face before, or since. I have never felt her arms wrap around me, before or since.

✳ ✳ ✳

'Dad.' Robert is the first to notice his presence. 'Come in. Sit down.'

He remains standing in the door way. 'I remember when she wrote that,' he tells them. 'It was such a long time ago. She put it in a competition about coming of age. But they said it wasn't meant to be about that sort of coming of age.'

He pauses and sighs. Struggling with how much he should tell.

'Your mother did come from a very unusual family. She didn't like to talk about her family, but her mother and father and older sister all seemed to live in their own separate worlds, not talking much, not touching, no friends, no other family. There was very little love. Right from when she was little your mother knew she was different from them.'

His words drop into the empty space between his adult children. No-one dares to look.

Except Robert. 'Sit down, Dad. Come and sit here,' he says as he pats the empty cushion beside him on the three seater.

His father walks over and sinks into the soft feather lounge.

'So tell us, Dad,' Robert asks him gently, 'How did she get out of there?'

His father looks around, taking his time.

'She left school at 15 and got a job at a bank and as soon as possible moved into a flat with some of the other girls who worked there.'

'And how did you get to meet her?' Robert asks.

'The girls all loved dancing and they would go every Saturday night to the local RSL club. I was pretty shy and thought I could meet a nice girl if I went along to the dances even though I was hopeless at it. When I saw her, looking so pretty, chatting and laughing with her friends, I thought that this was the girl I was going to marry. This was the mother of my children.'

He pauses for breath. 'It was much later that she started to talk about her ice. She called it that. She said that my loving was slowly melting it. She used to say that if she pretended to love me back, one day she would stop pretending and the loving would be real. And she was right. It was like that.'

He stops talking.

None of them break the quiet. They wait, knowing that he is not finished.

But he is. He stands up, dusts off his hands. 'Goodnight'.

A flat chorus of 'goodnight Dad' as they watch him shuffle out of the room.

Jennifer is the first to break the silence. 'So now we know why she never talked about her own family, her mum, or dad or big sister. Never being cuddled. Never feeling loved. Well that explains a lot.'

'What do you think it explains?' Andrew asks.

'What I mean,' Jennifer struggles, 'is that she found it hard hugging and cuddling me. I always felt it. The distance. But I can remember that she wasn't like that with you two,' she said, looking straight at me and Andrew.

Andrew lets out a long breath and recrosses his legs. Carol wonders if she should feel guilty especially when Jennifer adds, 'I always felt that I was being left out in the cold.'

Robert breaks the uncomfortable silence that follows. 'Well, I don't remember ever feeling unloved by her. She wasn't so much into cuddles, but then some mums aren't, are they? Later on she was sure there when I really needed her.'

Carol looks up at Jennifer, wondering if this explains why Jennifer didn't talk about her own children. Wondering how come they were in boarding school.

Andrew shuffles in his chair uncomfortably. Carol sends him a shrug – like we couldn't help getting the mum who softened with each baby. But that isn't the main thing on Andrew's mind at all.

'Look,' he says. 'just don't go there with theories that I am gay because our mum had a frigid mother and she was a bit uptight herself. Just don't. And anyway,' he adds, 'like Jennifer says, she wasn't frigid for me.'

Robert learns forward. 'It's OK mate,' and quickly adds, 'Do you all remember how she did everything for us. Just like the other mums. Perhaps even more so. But,' he muses out loud, 'you have to wonder at that little kid with the skates, and her racing so hard and lying to her parents about it. That's pretty brave.'

'Well we don't really know if that story was all true.'

We all looked at Andrew as he adds, 'We don't know how much was made up, do we?'

Jennifer cuts in. 'No we don't. But it was her story. She wrote it. Dad has just told us about her family. How much more truth do you want?'

'I wonder,' says Robert, 'if she told Dad not to tell us when her cancer got really bad. I wonder if she didn't want us to know or to see her life slipping away so suddenly. I wonder if she wanted us to remember her as strong and coping and always there when we needed her.'

His sentence hangs there.

Robert gives up on any more talk about their mother. Andrew retreats to feeling tetchy without really knowing why. Jennifer feels vindicated about feeling unloved.

Carol is the only one who wants to keep talking. That story and what her dad had just told them opens a whole new slant on their mother. She wants to explore it with them. How it has affected each of them. How it has affected their father. How it has affected the way they parent. She wonders if she conveniently got too busy to give as much love and attention to Jonah and Brook as they needed.

Robert jumps up.

'Wonder what's on TV?'

Jennifer sends another text to John and puts her phone down. Andrew sits there sending long messages all the way to the USA.

That night Carol rejects the temptation of another sleeping pill. She sizes up the single bed and wonders how on earth she used to sleep in it every night. Her body feels too large and unwieldy for this narrow space. It just won't fit any more. When she stops fidgeting for a few moments, she notices that the room has the faintest whiff of the familiar smell of old books, furniture polish and salt in the still night air. She half closes her eyes and pictures her Bob Dylan poster on the far wall, her hockey stick in the corner and rumpled clothes poking out from the chest of drawers. If she put her hand out she could touch the hopes and fears and fantasies that had whirled around her in this room, in this bed. Her adult self catches the memories of the adolescent Carol, wanting so much to be good but being the only one to keep failing to be good, no matter how hard she tried. Her parents being called to the school. Again. It's Carol. The nights she didn't come home from parties, driving her parents into a frenzy. The boys they never met and would never have approved of.

Carol squirms as she remembers it didn't stop with adolescence. Her moving up north on a crazy impulse and not even showing up to collect her degree. Falling in love. Having babies. Falling out of love. Poverty. Struggling back to work. Getting it together.

Lying there she lets in an old recurrent memory that still visits her, even after such a long time. That time when she found a newborn baby with its little cord still attached. Hearing its cries in the coastal bush, and following the sounds with her torch light. Expecting a hurt animal or bird. Never dreaming that she would come upon this. She remembers she had done something so unlike her, hanging out for some junk food, stopping for a Mac Burger, and then hating the smell of it in her car, tossing the packages out the window into the coastal scrub. And then she had braked and reversed, determined to find her rubbish. Hearing the sound. A persistent squawk. Sweeping around following the light of her torch. Then finding it. A newborn baby and only just warm to the touch, and how she had wrapped it in a towel, rubbed it warm and called the police. She smiles as she remembers they believed her when she said she had to stop for a pee and heard the sound. She did not want to hand the baby over. She wanted to keep that baby so that she could start all over again and do it better. She especially wanted to do it better with her teenage Brook. She so wanted right that moment to love Brook better.

Now she talks to her mother in the dark bedroom. She tells her mother that things did change after the baby. Brook started opening up more and told her about taking her best friend for an abortion and how they both felt so sad about not having the baby. Brook had told her that she understood that Carol didn't want to give the baby up to the police.

And Carol tells her absent mother that things had got so much better between her and Brook after that. She asks her if she had moments when things got better with each of her children. She asks her how on earth she managed her, when she, Carol, was that revolting teenager.

And she has no idea why she is telling her absent mother about that abandoned baby now, tonight, in her old bedroom, while her mother couldn't possibly hear her, not while she is slowly turning into a little pile of hot ashes. It hits her that there is no real mother to tell stuff to anymore. She lies there knowing that she never did tell her much at all and now it is too late.

Her mind floats back to the Ice story and her mother as a love-deprived child. How would it be growing up in that family? How did they all get like that? How did she break out of that mould? Why didn't her father fall in love with someone more normal? And how about that sister of hers? Did she inherit some weird gene from one or both their parents? Is it in the family? Have my children got it? Do I have it? Is it just sitting there in its recessive state, ready to jump out in my children's children? And why ice skating? She never took us ice skating. If she loved it so much why didn't she ever do it?

As Carol tosses the light blanket off and then pulls it up again, she can hear house noises of her siblings. One going to the toilet. One going down to the kitchen. Doors opening and closing. The house is alive with all of them noisily digesting, processing, disbelieving, rejecting, chewing over all that their father had told them and all that their mother had written.

Carol's pre-dawn thoughts turn to Jennifer and she tries to put herself in Jennifer's shoes. Being the eldest and having to be so sensible? How about having to watch out for the little kids when you know that they got the better deal? Did she have enough of little kids? Is that why she let them go to boarding school?

By morning Carol is worrying about the stuff. Sorting all the stuff. Jennifer with the biggest pile, Robert taking whatever Jennifer rejects, Andrew looking at his smaller pile of childhood stuff and wondering out loud how he is going to get it back home. And her with virtually no stuff. Perhaps they are all doing more than sorting stuff. Perhaps they are sorting out themselves. What does that say about her? She knows she has plenty to sort out. It's not normal to want nothing and to head off for a swim instead like a naughty teenager? Is that what she still is?

Finally Carol wonders about transfer of trauma through the generations. She wonders how much damage they all carry from their mother's dysfunctional family. How about that big unknown, her dad's past? That's still a big fat zero. What are they all carrying from that? A crushing sadness overwhelms her. She does not know her siblings' children and they don't know hers. There is a distance they all maintain. And now their father slips around like a ghost. He is totally unreachable in his solitary sadness.

Finally, she curls up, puts her thumb in her mouth and with the pointer finger of her other hand she twirls the fringe of her hair and falls asleep.

The hot sun pouring in through the window wakes her. She frees herself from the tangle of sheets, jumps us and indulges in the longest of hot showers.

FOUR

Over breakfast, they are all subdued. Carol says she had a bad night. A few nods. Their silence silences her. They get in each other's way, rinsing plates, stacking the dishwasher, wiping down the table.

'Hey.' It's Andrew. 'Let's all pile in the cars and go with Dad down to the beach house. He says he's moving down there. The least we can do is see what needs doing to the old place.'

It takes barely an hour, and they are piled into two cars heading south.

A few days of scraping, sanding, painting, scrubbing, and hosing down the outside and each other. Endless trips to the pitifully inadequate hardware store, lining up a handyman to finish the jobs they foolishly thought they could do. Pizza on the beach at sunset, and cricket games on the flat sand way past when it is too dark to see the ball.

At times their dad sits on the front verandah, his eyes closed to the sun, the hint of a smile on his face as he half listens to their chatter, the banging and the scraping and at times the shrieks of laughter as they slip back into adolescence and further back to endless summer childhood games. Andrew squirting everyone with the hose. Carol moving the ladder while Andrew is on the roof. Robert slipping away to catch up on the cricket score and forgetting to come back outside.

Over dinner their dad says he can remember one summer when Mum bought a plastic water slide and they put it down on the grass slope in the backyard and sprinkled bubble bath detergent all over it and ran the hose from the bore for hours, and all the neighbourhood children joined in, sliding and crashing till the bottom of the back yard was a slushy muddy mess and they all needed cold tea on their sunburnt shoulders. Yeah, Jennifer could remember that one too especially when their mother shooed everyone off so that she could have a turn too.

The moments of euphoria they share on the coast fade fast, as they pile into the cars to drive back to Sydney.

Once home, Jennifer, Robert and Andrew rummage around for extra bags to pack their excess luggage. Robert finds a courier of sorts on the net to take his back home.

On that last day in Sydney, Jennifer and Carol clean up the kitchen together. They empty out the cupboards and give them a good scrub, both in their own little scrubbing worlds, when Jennifer breaks the silence.

'I've been thinking of you and how you spent so much time protesting against logging in the forests and I really can't get a handle on what the problem was.'

Carol wants to scream out 'What?' Instead, she tries a patient explanation. 'Well it's old growth native forest and there's not all that much of it left. It was being logged illegally. Even by State Forests.'

That said, Carol pokes her head well into the bottom of a cupboard, stretching out to reach the old crumbs in the corners.

'Well, John's great grandfather and all the other farming pioneers spent years of their lives cutting down trees and pulling out stumps so that we could grow food. What's the matter with that?'

Carol is struggling. She backs out of the cupboard on her knees, and slowly stands up. 'True Jen,' she says. 'And thanks to them we now have lots of cleared areas to grow food. Same back home with the early dairy farmers.' She goes on, 'But that's very different from clearing the last bits of old growth native forests for wood chips.'

'For Japan,' she mutters to herself.

'So, we need paper.'

Carol brings out the big one. 'Not from old growth native forest. Not when there's hardly any left. Not when it's home to native birds and animals. Not when we need them to soak up some of that carbon dioxide we keep pumping into the air.'

'Crops and pasture soak up carbon too.'

Carol searches for a final bullet. She stands up straight, trying to look as tall as Jennifer. Trying to look her straight in the eye. She says to her sister's back, 'It's about biodiversity as well.'

'Never did get that biodiversity stuff.'

Carol eyes off their work.

'It looks like we've just about done every cupboard in this kitchen. Oh Jen, you've even done the drawers while we were talking.'

＊ ＊ ＊

On their last night after the last take-away, they struggle to find more to say to each other. Andrew asks Jennifer to sing. He finds an old guitar Jennifer has saved for the twins, and he strums and improvises to her voice. Their dad hovers. They sing songs they remember from their mother. Their dad walks back to his study.

Jennifer, Robert and Andrew leave early the next day. They say their goodbyes with a lot more love than their hellos just one week before.

And then there is just Dad and Carol.

'I'm going too, Dad, but I'll be back very soon. I want to come down the south coast with you. I don't want to live in the shack with you. I just want to be near you. I want to get to know you again.'

'You don't think I can manage, do you? Anyway, you all have your own lives now. You have a job.'

'I can always get work. I always have.'

'Well, how about the children?'

'Dad, they've both grown up and left home.'

'But your friends.'

'Good friends keep. Dad, I just want to get to know you better, that's all.'

'You're afraid I'll get down there and die.'

'No Dad. I'm not afraid of you dying. I'm sure of that now.'

He looks at her. 'Me too,' he says. 'I'm not afraid of it either.'

And then the first smile appears at the corners of his mouth and his eyes twinkle like Carol remembered as a child.

'Well then, Girlie, you'll have to learn some proper fishing habits. No more creeping around grabbing buckets of live fish and tipping them back into the sea like when you were little.'

'No, Dad.'

FIVE

Andrew props himself up against the check-in counter, his body and mind exhausted from the time with the family. He longs to be on the plane, putting a huge ocean between them.

He pulls out the last of his Australian cash to pay for the excess luggage that he already regrets.

He remembers when he first left Sydney for the USA and the exhilaration of leaving everything behind. All he needed then was a few extra clothes, his passport and visa, his wallet and his unbelievably chunky first mobile phone.

He completes the security check and heads for his departure gate with very little time to spare.

Ah, the joys of business class. No knees under his chin for the long haul.

At last, the huge aircraft is out on the runway, accelerates and then takes off. He allows himself one last reckoning on his family. His old family. He can't wait to get back to his new one.

Jennifer. Andrew was genuinely pleased to catch up with Jennifer again. In a way she was part of his mothering. They used to joke that he had two mothers. She always looked out for him. Stood up for him when he was being teased. Walked him home from school when he was little. Listened to his stories. How curious, he thought, she was about the same age as Christopher is now, when he, Andrew, was little and he realised that there was no way that Christopher would take on any parenting of any sibling. Not that there was any chance of that anyway. Paul didn't want or need any children of his own, and the last thing he needed was another baby to share.

Andrew felt safe in the circle of Jennifer's predictability.

She is still so predictable. She has fulfilled all her childhood dreams. Owning a horse. Living on a farm. Studying nursing. Being in charge of the ward. Everyone tucked up in bed with all the right medication, all the right meals and a buzzer that worked in case they needed something. Andrew smiles as he thinks of Jennifer and John's children, and how when they were little they would have known exactly what day it was, what was for dinner, what they were allowed to play with and what was forbidden, and what they wanted to be when they grew up.

Andrew pulls himself up short and tells himself to get real. Jennifer is in deep shit. All the drought records have been broken and autumn has become a drawn-out summer. After working hard all your life how do you face the real possibility of poverty? Losing everything. And how does John cope knowing that all of this is happening on his watch. Pasture turning into bare cracked soil, empty dams and creeks running dry.

His fingers move to a recent mosquito bite on his ankle and he worries for a moment. Ross River fever moving south from Queensland. Mosquito borne viruses we hadn't even heard of.

He picks up the magazine that the air steward has handed out and flips through the promotional stories searching for something to catch his interest. Nothing. Onto his third small bottle of red wine, the tensions from the dash through the Sydney traffic are slipping away. He even smiles at the woman across the aisle. No use starting a conversation yet. There are still hours and hours to go and there's always the risk of starting up with someone who ends up being really boring and wanting to tell you all about their family or their job, or even worse, their relationship.

Andrew closes his eyes and lets his thoughts go random. They settle on his mother and her very private death. He wonders what else she kept private, tucked away, like nobody's business. Like her childhood. Like her parents. Never even met them. He recalls the 'Ice' story, and the sister and wonders if they were all really that weird? He thinks autism. Autism wasn't even known back then. He knows autism and kids on the spectrum from school. And yes there are some families where most of them are afflicted. But how about being the only one who isn't?

He recalls the big dining table of his childhood with all four of them sitting around it at night doing their homework, or perhaps with him and Carol just drawing. He sees their mother, sitting quietly with her knitting, ready to join in conversations, encouraging them, among the big mess of school books, paper, paste, coloured pencils. Sometimes the concentration was so intense you could feel it vibrating the very air they were breathing.

Their dad, out of the circle. Except when sitting with Robert, the two of them engrossed in complex maths. Andrew stirs uncomfortably in his seat. That old feeling. Not good enough. Never brilliant. Never good at sport. Definitely not Robert. Good enough for his mother, and always Jennifer's precious little brother, but never good enough for his dad.

He could hear his father's voice, 'You'll spoil that boy, Gabby. He gets his way far too often. You and Jennifer, like two clucky hens. You'll just make him soft.'

And he remembers all he felt was warm and loved by both of them. If that was spoiling, whatever that meant, then bring it on!

Andrew wonders if his dad believed that too much mothering made you gay. He wonders if his dad had any real understanding of how it was for him. Because he wasn't like the typical gay boy who always knew he preferred boys. He loved having girl friends while he was growing up and yet, at the same time, he could still look at boys with a kind of hunger. He wonders if his dad had any real grasp of the reality that he could fall in love with Lisa, share Christopher's birth like it was the most precious moment they would ever have in all of their lives, and then fall out of love with her. Lisa. Still good friends. Andrew smiles to himself. She understood. She let him go. Each so lonely at first. Each bravely sharing notes, sharing decisions, sharing Christopher himself. After all, was this freedom that neither of them really wanted? And then she met Leon. And then he met Paul.

Andrew ponders his bisexuality. It is a familiar ponder-habit. He finds it quite intriguing as he knows only a few people like him. He knows quite a few men who have been married and had kids and then admitted that they had been gay all along. And he knows women like that too, who settled for being a lesbian after marriage and kids. He likes exploring in his mind having a whole chain of relationships with men other than Paul. But then he thinks of Christopher. After all, he reminds himself, it must be challenging for a kid to spend his first eight years with a mum and dad, and then get shared between his dad and his new bloke and his mum and her new bloke especially when that bloke's two teenagers come to stay on random weekends and school holidays.

Andrew feels the familiar stab of missing Christopher. He's missed out a whole week and then some. He misses him the half week he's with Lisa. He can't wait to have him at home again all to himself. Somehow, on those half weeks, Paul finds that he has lots of extra work, needs to stay back at the office, have dinner with old friends. It works for them. Andrew is the father of this delicious child and Paul definitely is not.

Andrew grabs his phone and starts a text to Lisa. 'Arriving at 10am tomorrow morning your time. Thinking of dropping by and picking up Christopher if that is OK for you – if you don't have Saturday morning plans for him.' He was about to the press the send button and stopped.

Message to Paul. 'Missing you so much. Don't come to the airport in the dreadful Saturday morning traffic. I'll grab a taxi and we can have a wonderful day together. Will make arrangements to see Christopher Sunday.'

Sometimes, Andrew thinks as he rewrites Lisa's message, it's hard getting the right balance.

SIX

Jennifer gets on the plane for the short trip to Wagga and then the long drive home. She feels weighed down and out of pocket with all the extra luggage. That is not all that is weighing her down.

She plonks down on the aisle seat, carefully chosen so that she can get to the toilet without having to bother anyone else. She closes her eyes as a clear sign that she wants no conversation. She is thankful that the stock and station agent she recognises is many rows back from her.

There is that old familiar drag in her stomach. She knows it from childhood, all the way through her teenage years, and now here it is again. She feels very different from her siblings. She cannot enter the fun they seem to have with each other and even with their dad. Like when they were all horsing around at the beach house wetting each other with hoses. The game went on and on. Jennifer pretended to enjoy it, as she always had. She had pretended it was funny. But it wasn't.

Jennifer feels the bitter taste of resentment in her mouth. She could hear her mother's voice. 'Just watch the baby for a moment, love, while I put the clothes on the line.' 'Make sure Robert doesn't go near the oven.' 'There's a good girl, see if Carol will have a few more spoons-full of the veggies.' 'Come on, Jennifer, let her play with one of your dolls.' 'Can you see what Andrew is crying about?' 'Is Robert being too rough with him?' 'I don't know how on earth I would manage without my big girl!'

Well where was her big boy? Why didn't Robert have to take on some of this? When he was the age she had started minding him, he was minding no one. He wasn't even minding himself! She felt her own anger prickling behind her eyes and her throat going red. The way her father thought the sun shone out of Robert, just because he started talking so early, just because he could kick a ball so far as a toddler, just because he could run faster than any of them, just because he was a boy.

Jennifer remembers how her friends from school were so jealous that she had three such adorable little ones at home. They tried to hoist them up on one hip like Jennifer did but could never quite manage to keep them there like she could. No ledge. Well, she still had a ledge.

Sometimes, she remembers, she went out to play with her friends, instead of staying in after school to help her mum. She always wanted more. She wanted to go to their places after school every day. She wanted to put distance between herself and the little ones. When her dad came home and went straight to her for a kiss, and patted her on the head, and asked what his big girl was up to today, she knew it was all worthwhile. And in a way it was. They were adorable. When they were little. She did love them to bits.

But for goodness sakes, Jennifer tells herself. Now they are all adults. All equal. So why did she have to keep them on track, making sure they got through all that their dad had expected of them at the house. Forever moving it on. Calling them back from taking their various 'Time outs'. Back to sorting stuff out. Getting rid of all the unwanted things. Getting the beach house fixed up before they all had to leave. Staying focused. What was the matter with her? More to the point what was the matter with them?

Jennifer allows herself to go down that track. Well, we all know what is wrong with Robert. Psychosis. And what a cop-out that one is. After all, if only he would take his medication every day and get help at the first sign of hearing and seeing things, then he would be OK. Any nurse knows that. That's what medication is for. But no, he has to stuff his body around with cannabis and lord knows what else, and then he feels so chilled out, he thinks he can miss out a few days of tablets, and a few days more and before he knows it he is in a full blown episode and someone has to pick up the pieces. Well not me, Jennifer tells herself. She feels she has picked up enough pieces to last her a life time.

And then there is her spoilt little hippy sister. What a goodie goodie, putting her life on hold and going down to mind Dad. The best thing would be to let him get on with his life without Mum. He has his beloved beach shack. He can fish all day if he wants.

Jennifer feels another niggle of resentment rising.

And how about Carol's kids? Wouldn't you know they would have hippy jobs. Yes, of course, they were brought up 'in paradise', where just about everyone who had a job had it part-time so that they could indulge themselves in being a surfie or an ecoterrorist, or doing meditation circles, or yoga weekends or growing fucking organic vegetables in their over-grown permaculture gardens. Let them try to be real farmers. They'd soon find out what life is like when your kids' school fees depended on getting 500 hectares of wheat in at the right time, getting the cows pregnant at the right time, and when the whole bloody flock of sheep has to be moved around every week so that they have enough feed, and how you can't get shearers any more because the huge companies that owned the huge stations are offering them more to shear at their place at peak time and the big cotton farms upstream are taking too much water to store in their enormous damns. Hadn't they heard of evaporation? Hadn't they heard of sharing? What use were water rights when there wasn't any water?

And Andrew. Jennifer relaxes somewhat at the thought of Andrew. What a delicious baby he was. What a sweet little boy. What an angel who happily played by himself for hours. And how he broke into inconsolable sobs when his father had less praise for his music grades than if he had made the A cricket team. Jennifer hopes he is happy now. He seems happy with Paul, and seems to be doing a great job with Christopher. Jennifer couldn't quite get her head around how he could have been so happy at first with Lisa and now so happy with Paul. Oh, well.

Suddenly she is overcome with a fear so big and so sudden, she can hardly get out of her seat. She does not want to go home. She does not want to go back to John. There's no real contact anymore. He's far away, in his own despair. Unreachable. And now she doesn't even want to reach out.

She wants to be coming home to her children instead. She lets in the old familiar question of how she could have ever agreed to them going off to boarding school, just because it was what John's family had always done with their children. She recalls John saying that it hadn't done him any harm. Never game enough to reply, 'You reckon!'

She sits in the plane waiting for the queue to start moving and the memories flood back to long ago when there was just the two of them in the cottage. The best time of her life before she fell pregnant with the twins, and then John had joked that it was like saving on the vet's fees, having two for the price of one.

As she waits for her luggage to appear on the roundabout, she gets a flashback of the mare lying in the pool of blood. At least she'll soon be home to make sure the foal is OK.

Jennifer grabs a trolley for all of her luggage. Big arms sweep it off the roundabout and dump it down in front of her. She looks up.

'John.' She waits not knowing what to expect.

'All of this?'

'Afraid so.'

'Missed you luv. Don't go away again for a while, eh.'

She lets herself go soft into his big hug.

'Oh, and that little fella in the barn. You won't recognise him. He's grown so big.'

Shades of the old John. Jennifer is unsettled.

SEVEN

Carol now wakes each morning with the sun streaming through the easterly window of the tiny backyard beach cabin she has moved into. She relishes the light breeze blowing the sheer cotton curtains. She can turn her head and look down the driveway alongside the house that Clem and Dot Turner built before she was born. She can remember the Turner family and how their four boys used to play with them, the little O'Brien kids, teaching them how to catch prawns and crabs, how to skim stones over still water and how to cheat at Monopoly.

Carol can glance around this small one-room cabin and see everything that she needs to dress, feed and amuse herself. Not much. But not much feels good. She smiles as she pictures her rented house up north full of memorabilia from her adult life. Now, like her new part-time, casual job at the nearby rehabilitation centre, she feels everything in her life is part-time and casual.

Most mornings she wakes early and lies in bed letting her thoughts ramble. Frank and Gabrielle O'Brien. It's comforting to say their names out loud. Not so comforting to see them anew through adult eyes. Not so comforting to know there are no more conversations with her mother. No chance to get her talking about her childhood or to share conversations about the challenges of parenting. Woman to woman. All those people at the funeral. What did they really know of Frank and Gabrielle O'Brien? Did they just see a solidly predictable and reliable couple? And how solidly predictable and reliable have their grown up children been? Carol muses on this for a while. Jennifer. Same farm, same farmer. Same profession. Same hospital. Carol shudders at the thought.

Most mornings she struggles into her bathers, grabs a towel, shoves her feet into thongs at the doorstep and runs down the drive, past the Turner's old fibro cottage, across the road, across the grassy reserve to the sand, dumping things as she runs full speed into the water. She knows that if she slows down she won't stand a chance of getting wet. Even in summer the sea here is cold. The warmer currents that are definitely not warm don't come in till summer is almost over and only stay for a few brief months. She can't believe that they didn't notice the cold as children.

Carol's arms turn into a windmill, her legs kick with urgent spasms, she can feel her brain shrinking inside her head as she makes herself swim, over and under the waves, out into the bay, till the ice in her veins begins to thaw, and then she breast-strokes back, head up, facing the little row of cottages lined up on the shore. On a good day she catches a wave back to the sand, and lies there for a while, in the bubbly shallows, catching her breath. She runs the short distance home, wrapped up in her towel, clutching her thongs, and jumps into the hot outdoor shower behind the cabin. She watches as the blue patches on her legs turn to bright pink and she feels gloriously alive as her body warms up in the steamy sunlight. Hot. Cold. Hot. How she would love to roll in icy snow and then plunge into hot pools. How she would like to push the boundaries and see how cold she could actually go before her core turns into ice.

Everyone in this seaside village says she exaggerates how cold the water is. Nonsense. Her norm is the subtropical beaches close to the Queensland border. Her norm is ocean water that embraces your body with the faintest hint of coolness. Her norm for nearly all of her adult life has been summer for most of the year, with just a few months of needing a light blanket at night.

It has been a month now since Carol moved down to be near her dad. She is careful not to overcrowd him. They have settled on a routine that pretty much suits them both. Once a week Carol calls by for their bush walk and then she goes down to his place another afternoon for some work on the veggie garden he has started in his backyard. Like him, it is neat, exact and organised to perfection.

At first they worked on the garden in silence. He knew exactly what he wanted, doing his share of the grunt work as much as he could, and probably more than he should. She was glad she didn't see him the next morning trying to tie his shoe laces or easing himself into the car.

After their garden work, they would sit in dirty garden clothes on the front verandah, sipping beer and eating the casserole she has brought.

'The house sold last Monday,' he starts off.

'Dad, that was quick. It had only been on the market for a few weeks.'

'Yeah. Those stupid agents would have had me doing it all up and filling it with rented furniture and knick-knacks but I put my foot down and said that anyone looking for a good family home would be able to see what it looked like with its own furniture. Anyway it did sell, straight off, and at a much higher price that I thought possible.'

'So how do you feel about that?'

He looks at her, as if to say that was a really stupid question.

'Well, Girlie, I'm relieved to be rid of it. No use for it now, is there?'

He is quiet for a while and then says, 'I've got plenty of Super to live on now. More than I need. I want to share the proceeds of the house with you all. Divide it five ways. I'll keep a bit in case I out-live my usefulness and need to get some care, but I want you all to get your share now. It's no use waiting till I die.'

Carol lets 'die' go unanswered.

'Dad, are you sure? Do you want to get some advice about this?'

'Of course I'm sure. But I need to talk to Robert. That boy knows he's not well, and we might have to put some away in a trust for him, so that he can get what he needs, but can't get his hands on it while he is having one of his bad spells. I need to sort it all out before I distribute it to you others.'

'Yes, of course. No rush.'

Her Dad puts his hands down flat on the table, as he does every night that she can remember at the end of the evening meal, signalling that he was about to stand up and leave the table for the TV news. But he has a new habit.

'Got to go and skype that boy of Andrew's before he has to get ready for school. He's got a new app he wants to tell me about.'

This is her signal to give him a hug, which he relaxes into for a second or two, before he says, 'My dishes.'

'OK. Goodnight then Dad.'

'Thanks.' He always adds, 'Your mother would be proud of you.'

Carol walks away so that he doesn't see the tears welling up. How she has always wanted her mother to be proud of her. But funny how she always did everything she could to push that to the limit. Always dodging helping around the house. Staying out late and not telling them where she was. But deep down, Carol feels that her mother had a special love for her wild child. She remembers her mother's hand would linger at bed time, when she bent down to tuck Carol in and kiss her forehead, and her fingers would stroke Carol's hair, and she would breathe soft hush, hushes, to relax her tight and energetic little body, and Carol would slide into sleep, safe in a soft cocoon of being loved.

EIGHT

The sale of the family house is niggling at Carol's brain. Like her dad, she doesn't feel that she needs money at the moment. It's Robert that is bugging her. She's not all that happy with her dad's idea of just talking to Robert about it. What if Robert appeared to be OK when they started talking about it but was not really OK? What if he objected strongly to being treated differently from the rest of them? What if he got the money and then, on a whim, gave it away, or got into a relationship with a woman who thought he was a soft touch? And what did her dad know about trusts? Probably a bit, but probably not enough. And would her dad get the advice he needed?

She thinks of the only lawyer she knows. Jack Turner. Son of Dot and Clem. When she was looking for somewhere to live, the local agent contacted Jack, who remembered the O'Brien family and was delighted that Carol might be interested in the cabin.

She knows that Jack lives in Sydney and teaches law at the university. It seems he is the only Turner boy who uses the beach house. Since Carol moved in Jack has come down for a few weekends, each time with a group of blokes. Not much conversation with her. Just 'You settled in OK?'

'Yes thanks.'

'That's good.'

'Yes.'

Last week they had a whole conversation

'You still settled in OK?'

'Oh yes. I just love it here. Dad's just down the road, and I can keep an eye on him.'

'Sorry to hear about your mum. I lost both of my parents a few years back.'

'That must have been hard.'

'Mmmm. Well glad to have someone using the cabin.'

And then he added that next time he was coming down just by himself. That he was taking some leave and wanted to fix up the place a bit. And that perhaps they could go out for a meal together, or something.

Carol thought that could be a good idea. Perhaps, if they got on OK, she might be able to ask him about legally protecting mentally ill people from wasting away their inheritance.

✳ ✳ ✳

Carol can see her dad slowly edging himself out of his grief and back into some sort or routine. He lets drop that his old fishing mates have been around, tempting him to join them in their old tinny, when the tide is right, the moon is right, the wind is right and none of the four of them are down with ills and complaints or hangovers. Surprisingly they go at least one night a week.

The postmistress tells her that he has been sighted at the Old Timers Old Time Dancing at the local RSL and that he is in much demand as a still-standing still-moving older male with no obvious bad smells or habits. She can't wait to let the others know about that.

He's started to talk to her more about some articles he has been reading. When they watch the news together he is back to his old tricks of shouting at the TV for its insane choice of news items and rants at the politicians who are ruining the state and the whole country, not to mention the world. Aware of the line that she dares not cross, Carol doesn't ask him if he has found a good local doctor or if he is on any medication or if he wants her to check out any specialists in the regional centre. She is mindful that she is not his minder. If not that, she sometimes wonders what exactly she is there for.

Slowly he is opening up to her. As they re-explore the coastal national parks that border the village, he starts his reminiscences. She is the witness to his past, that even more than the present, weighs heavily on him. The only things that slow him down are the uphills.

It began during the very first bush-walk they took together. The autumn weather was, at last, getting chilly at night, while the days were still warm. Perfect for walking. She deliberately chose a fairly flat walk through the coastal scrub. Sparse with trees. Lots of flowering shrubs. The ever present sound of the waves breaking on the beaches, and the occasional view of the sea on the slight rises.

For a while now he has talked about Gabbby and why she left home so young, and why they both lost contact with their families. He talks about their determination to be strong, for the children. He talks about how it didn't always work out that way. Sometimes it's as if he's talking to himself, and sometimes he gets surprised to find that Carol has been by his side the whole time. But mostly he wants to tell it, and he wants her to hear it. It's been unspoken for far too long.

Carol makes notes when she gets home, and sometimes she checks the details on the next walk, to see if she has got it right, or prompts him to follow up where he left off. She is a repository for long held secrets. She feels like a voyeur peeping through the greenery at the past. Not just her mother's past, but lately hints of his childhood too. She hears, in drawn out instalments, the harm that each of her parents had endured. She hears it all, and doesn't want to hear it all. There is a strange new bond forming between her and her father, and she feels that she has grown in status from the grown up child to the grown up person. He trusts her. She wants more, about him.

'Dad, what was it like for you when you were growing up?'

At first he is slow and thoughtful and Carol is concerned that he is struggling to start talking, but then he gets into a rhythmic walking pace and it all comes tumbling out, with him looking far ahead as they walk, as if he is telling it all to the distance and she is just looking on from the side.

'When I was a little critter, my dad was away in the Vietnam war. Apparently he'd been in the army for some years so he went as an older enlisted soldier. My mother and I moved in with her parents until I was about four years old. Grandad gave me an electric train set and Grandmother let me help her cook and garden. Well I suppose I wasn't really any help at all but she certainly made me feel like I was. My mother went to work during the day. She and I shared a bedroom in their little house.'

Carol waits for him to catch his breath and go on.

'Then my father came home. He'd saved enough from his pay to buy a piece of farming land in the western district. He was anxious to move there and start his farm, so he had an old house delivered on a truck from Queensland. He went out there first to make sure it was properly settled on its footings, and that the rain ran from the roof into the corrugated iron water tank and that the generator worked the lights. I was sad to leave my grandparents' house. I didn't know where I was going or what my father was like. But I had my mother and my grandparents promised to visit us soon.'

He paused again. Thinking. Waiting for the words to match his memories.

'My first memories out there were of being lonely and having no one to play with. Both my mother and father were busy getting the house organised and the farm ready for cattle. They took me out with them to fix up the fences and gates. I made up games in the dirt, with stones and bits of dried grass. My father bought an old tractor and they spread lots of grass and clover seed, hoping for rain so that the dry paddocks would turn into pasture. But it didn't rain much. Well, not enough, anyway. Never enough. Except when we had floods, when the Darling River spread out wide even up to our farm house and locked us in for weeks on end. My father could only afford a small herd of cattle. It was always a struggle.'

Frank comes to a stop startled by the totally different land-scape they just walked into. They see the legacy of last year's coastal bush fires that had raged with record temperatures. The floor of what had been the forest is charred black, and small tufts of grass and shoots are a striking lime green against the black. All the undergrowth had been burnt away, revealing the bones of the landscape, clusters of giant boulders, and they can see the rising and falling of the land into smalls hills and valleys. Gone is the camouflaged ground cover of leafy shrubs, ferns and grasses. It is startlingly naked.

Frank says he remembers many bush fires in this part of the coast, but never one that has been so fierce.

'What is it, Girlie?' he asks, 'Is it true the that the fires are getting hotter?'

Carol liked that he expected she would know the answer to that.

'Well, it's getting warmer and wetter and so there is more undergrowth to burn. More fuel, hotter fires. Yes it's true.'

'It's all changing,' he says. 'The bush used to go right down to the beach. Now there are houses built where there used to be sand dunes. The fishers tell me we need those dunes. They stop the big waves from the Christmas-tides from washing into the town.'

'And have they done that? Have they washed into town?'

'I've not seen it. But I've heard about it.'

The walked on, Frank leading. Carol was trying to imagine her Dad as a child, out in the bush with only his parents for company. She waited till they had gone through the burnt area of coastal forest and suggested they rest for a while but he kept walking. She sped up so as to walk next to him.

'You were telling me about moving out to the farm with your parents.'

'Where was I up to?'

'Your mum and dad and the struggle they had setting up the farm.'

'Are you sure you want to know about this. It's so long ago.'

Carol nodded. 'Go on.'

He took a deep breath. 'I think the drinking started gradually. When things went wrong, he got drunk. Like when the tractor ran out of fuel and he had to walk home for hours in the hot sun. And when he got drunk, he got mean and angry. I could hear them at night. My mother trying to stay out of his way, or soothe him with soft talking, but more often it would end with her stifling a scream and I could hear his fist make contact with her body, sometimes soft, sometimes hard, fist hitting bone. And then he would take off into the night and not come back for a day or two. My mother was pretty quiet during those times. I had to promise her not to tell anyone, but I had no-one to tell anyway.'

They found a smooth rock ledge and Carol suggested they sit down for a while. She took from her backpack a bottle of water and dried fruit and nuts which they ate in silence, till he stood up ready to walk on. She suggested they turn back so they set off again through the charred landscape.

Frank was back to his story, the rhythm of his walking matching his way of talking.

She heard about the long bus ride to the nuns' school in the nearest town. She heard about him having very few friends, about his bed wetting till he was nine, and the long walk from the front gate where the bus dropped him so that sometimes it was dark by the time he got home.

She heard about how he always came top of the class and about how proud his mother was and how even his father would pat him on the head with a 'Well done, boy'.

But the most difficult thing for her to hear was his entrenched fear for his mother and his fear of getting hurt himself, and how, as he grew into adolescence, he dreamed of getting bigger and stronger than his father so he could fight back, so he could see his father begging him to stop as he felt his knuckles striking the bones of his face.

'What saved me was getting a scholarship to board at the big Catholic boys' school in Dubbo.'

'But I kept to myself,' he added, 'I could never tell them about my father, and I couldn't ever get it out of my head that my mother was still out there, with him.'

Carol nodded.

'I got another church scholarship to go to university in Sydney. Part of me didn't want to go, but I guess a bigger part did, just to get away from everything.'

'After all that help from the church, did you believe in God?' she asked. 'Did you pray? For your mother?'

'No, Girlie,' he said. 'Although I did get close to thanking God when Dad rolled the tractor and got trapped under it.'

'What happened?'

'Mum thought he was off on one of his benders, so he died there.'

No more prompting. How could she say 'how sad,' when it wasn't really sad. Not for her father then or now in his telling of it. She tried to imagine what it could possibly be like, to be thankful that one of your parents had died. She looked at him, standing there in the woods, gnome like, and felt a rush of love towards him, being acutely aware of his mixture of old determination and new fragility and was tearfully grateful he was still here.

As they sat there, with no need for more conversation, she promised herself to set aside some time to think more about their dad and his childhood. She know it wasn't such an extraordinary story. She knew that there were plenty of stories like that with war veterans, but it was extraordinary because it was her dad, and none of his children had any idea.

Frank stood up, 'You ready for the rest of it? Might as well finish what we've started, eh Girlie?'

She nodded, pleased to see ahead the cleared land that ran alongside the beach. She prompted, 'So what happened to your mother after he died?'

'Mum sold the farm, paid out the bank mortgage and moved into Dubbo, but she wasn't really capable of looking after herself. I don't know if she was brain damaged from too many blows, but she went into some sort of home and died soon after. It's never left me, you know, that feeling that I should have saved her from him.'

Carol wanted to tell him that she thought he was amazing to have come through that. She wanted to thank him for being able to be such a beautiful gentle father, who indeed never laid a hand on any of them. She wanted to tell him that it was not OK for his mother to have suffered, that it was not his fault that he didn't know how to save her.

But she didn't say any of those things.

'It must have left its own scars on me, too,' he went on. 'I got my degree and a good job. I saved up and bought a house. But I was lonely. I wanted friends and most of all I wanted a girlfriend. Finally I got up the courage to go to the local dances. And that's where I was lucky enough to meet your mother.'

He stood still and was silent for a while, and then looked at her with a face so drained she feared for him.

'Oh Dad, thank you so much for telling me all of this. It's strange though,' she added, 'that you kept it all to yourself.'

'She knew,' he said. 'Gabby knew about me, and I knew about her, and somehow that was enough.'

'Mm.'

'We didn't see any reason for telling you children about this. Why would we? If we kept it all to ourselves then sometimes we could pretend none of it ever happened.'

They were back in the main street. He turned to her.

'Next time you can do the talking, Girlie.'

But next time he got sick and it wasn't till a few weeks later that he was able to go on long walks and talk at the same time.

NINE

Robert is woken up too early by a strange noise in the garden. The sun isn't quite up yet. He lifts one corner of the curtains and peeps out. Bloody brush turkey scratching around in the dirt under his window. Robert puts the pillow over his head and goes back to sleep.

He sits on the verandah like he does every morning, in the same chair, with strong black coffee and two slices of well-done toast and enough peanut butter so that it sticks to the roof of his mouth. He lets it take its own time to ooze slowly onto his tongue.

He likes to look up to the tops of the tall ancient camphor laurel trees and watch for summer breezes. He thinks of China and the masses of people there right now, two billion of them. His mind moves away from the global population explosion and the ever haunting questions of not enough water and food to go around. He imagines how it will get really ugly with unimaginable droughts and famines and rising waters that flood the prime agricultural estuaries and coastlines. Robert forces himself to focus instead on the smell of the camphor wood box that lived in his parents' house in the big hall outside the bathroom and how the towels that were stored in it smelt just like the camphor leaves today. He notices the brush turkey nearby gathering the fallen camphor leaves. He closes his eyes and breathes deeply that nostalgic smell that penetrates deep inside him.

The commotion at his feet startles him into wakefulness. The brush turkey has moved into a manic mode, using its feet to sweep all the mulch that Robert has carefully spread on the garden beds. The mulch is travelling at great speed onto the big pile at the corner of the verandah. Robert knows the signs well. This is the beginning of a brush turkey nest, and it has a very long way to go.

The brush turkey does not stop to feed, to drink or to rest. It methodically bares the earth from the long garden bed against the house. Every scrap of mulch gets added to the growing pile. All the leaves that have dropped on the path are added.

Robert continues to sit there, his eyes fixed on the turkey. Eventually the turkey stops and makes eye contact. Robert hears it say, 'I can't do this on my own. I need you to stay there and keep watch. I can't build this nest and chase away any strange bird bloke that comes in here and starts claiming the nest as his own. And the neighbour's dog. You have to keep it away. Right?'

'Fair enough,' says Robert, but the bird has already turned its back for the next load of mulch and leaves.

Robert goes inside and checks the kitchen. He makes a list. He checks the bathroom and laundry supplies and adds soap powder. He gets on line and checks his bank balance and then goes onto the site for the Woolworths store in town and sends an order that should keep him going for at least a month. He pays extra for home delivery. That just about cleans out his bank account.

Robert makes himself another cup of coffee and sits back down on the old lumpy verandah chair, preparing himself to wait out the duration. He has his laptop and looks up how long brush turkeys take to build a nest. He settles back in the chair that has seen better days in posh living rooms, and feels the family of mice that now call it home running up and down inside the upholstery. He feels their little bodies massaging his shoulders causing them to tingle. He tries to get the mice to focus on his spine, but they have their own agenda, and today, shoulders will just have to do.

As the days grow longer, Robert finds himself spending more and more time on the verandah. The brush turkey is tireless as the nest mound grows. It is now over three metres in diameter and half as high. Robert hopes it is nearly complete as the brush turkey is looking decidedly wasted. He has lost a significant amount of weight. His tail feathers, once a fine collection of shiny black plumes have moulted down to a pathetic few wisps. When he needs a break from his work, he twitches. Any suggestions from Robert that he helps with the mound are met with a resounding 'NO!' Robert feels rejected. After all he has put his life on hold. He has kept guard and fended off the dogs. Fortunately there have been no other male turkeys around.

At last the brush turkey puts the finishing touches to the mound. He struts around it with all the pride and sexual appeal he can manage. Soon after a female brush turkey appears. She approaches the mound and inspects it very carefully. He waits. She walks to the top and scratches round with her beak. Robert thinks she is being haughty. She doesn't do gratitude. She does business. Robert thinks he'll leave them alone for a bit to sort it out and goes in for a long shower and his evening meal. When he comes back, in the fading daylight, there she is. Sitting on the top like a queen. The exhausted king is nowhere to be seen.

A few days later the queen takes some time out leaving him back in control of the nest. Every morning and evening the poor male bird arrives for mound duty. As it is slowly packing down with the heat of decomposition, he adds more mulch, which is a big ask as he has to go quite a long way to find it now. Robert has taken to leaving little piles closer but he ignores this gesture. 'Not your business, Robert.' Then there is temperature control. A slow and thorough reading with the beak plunging into the top where the eggs now lay submerged, and an adjustment of leaves off or leaves on depending on the reading.

Robert is still on watch, especially for dogs. The female bird has not come back. She's flipped off. It's all up to him now, the father. Now that the main work is over, he's putting on a little weight and condition but he is still twitchy. Seeing hatching through is obviously taking its toll. Robert is feeling grateful that he has given fatherhood a miss.

Another month and Robert happens to be present for the great event. A slow turbulence at the top of the mound. And then one, two, six little bald heads appear, followed by bodies covered with a sparse fluff. Little eyes squint at the strong sunlight. Robert goes inside to get his camera. He gets distracted by checking the photos that are already there.

When he returns the chicks have gone. The father has gone too. And the mother, well she never came back. He feels bereft, deserted, abandoned. All he is left with is a big messy mound of rotting leaves, bare garden beds, an extra layer of fat around his middle and a very low bank balance.

He feels it coming. It starts deep in his stomach, the strong inward pull of an impending tidal wave of grief. It creeps up from behind. It crashes down on his back, his shoulders, and penetrates through his skin into muscle and down into his bones and guts. He doubles over and howls in acute emotional pain.

She's gone. She's never coming back. She has left us and we didn't even say goodbye.

He waits it out till it slowly passes and he watches as the wave of sorrow moves down the garden to the dirt road on its way to the next poor bastard.

It could be time to pay his big sister a visit.

TEN

Carol catches herself thinking about Robert a lot these days. His mental illness absorbs her. She wonders if there is some inherent family gene that she should be vigilant about. She wants to quiz her children about how they are coping with life. But of course she doesn't. Perhaps, she thinks, she should be quizzing herself instead.

Robert was the big brother she adored. That wasn't surprising. Everyone adored Robert. He had a classically gorgeous face, with his piercing blue eyes, and he was more than good at just about everything. Their parents were so proud of him. But for Carol, he was her guardian angel. He would read her stories and listen to her rantings about the complex politics of the girls' playground. He took her to her first movie, *The Sound of Music*. Mum and Dad trusted that he would look after her and he did, even waiting outside the ladies' toilet at the cinema, when she needed a pee in the middle of the movie.

For Carol it is almost inconceivable that he would be the one. That his charmed boyhood held the secret of his tortured future. How could that be? How could that be lurking inside the sporting hero, the dux of the school, the one out of all of them who made their dad so proud and their mum's heart sing.

Depression hit Robert at eighteen. Actually Robert's depression hit them all when he was eighteen. Suddenly the house was strewn with egg shells. Do not upset him. Do not upset Mum. Do not upset Dad. Full blown psychosis didn't hit for another five years and by that time, Jennifer had finished her nursing and was working out west at country hospitals,

Carol had gone north on a hippie dream of communal living and Andrew, well, the little brother had gone overseas and was not coming back.

Carol is learning that her father needs to talk about Robert but he can't talk about him for long. So she is finding out bits and pieces that she is trying to fit together. A secret hell her parents were plunged into. Frightening episodes. Suicide attempts. Prison. All glossed over at the time. 'Oh, he's doing as well as can be expected.' That was their mantra.

Guilt is weighing down on her, guilt that she just went on with her own life, not offering to come down to Sydney when Robert was especially ill, not inviting him to her place for a while, not questioning her parents more closely as to what was really going on. Wanting to believe that everything was alright.

'He's alright – the rehab is the best place for him.' 'He's alright, he's just out of town at the moment, visiting an old school friend.'

And the few times he was at home when she visited, she recalls, he was overweight and untidy, distracted and oh so weary. She wonders now how on earth she could have been hoodwinked into believing that he was alright. Well, she guessed, compared to how he was when he was full blown psychotic, he was alright.

As her dad lets slip the bits of the puzzle, she keeps hearing over and over in her head, 'We all fled and our parents were left to cope with the whole disaster.'

Carol sometimes dwells on this when she is walking along the beach in the early evenings. Other local beach walkers see her striding into the wind with tears streaming down her face. They leave her be. Word gets around. They know she has just lost her mother.

As she walks, Carol is recreating the scenes as they should have been played. She's reciprocated his care and attention to her as a child. She's been with him during the darkest times. She has listened attentively to whatever he wants to tell her. And she has given her parents time out. 'You don't have to do this all by yourselves. We can share it. After all, it's family.'

But for now, Carol reminds herself, her role is to be the receiver of these family stories in those times when her dad needs to unload. In his own way. In his own time. Little bits pop out. There is no sequence. There is no beginning and middle. There is no focusing on what has helped Robert and what has not. Carol types it all up in her laptop, and puts the main points on big post-its. She sticks them on the wall and moves them around when she gets another piece of the puzzle.

Robert has been in court twice. Once he got a warning with a good behaviour bond and the second time he served four months. That was for breaking into a neighbour's backyard and tossing all the expensive outdoor furniture plus the barbeque and bar fridge into the pool.

Frank says he finds it really frustrating that while Robert does go crazy at times, he still gets tried in a court of law as if he is perfectly sane all of the time. He knows what he is doing. He knows it is wrong. He is very contrite. He pleads guilty. He admits that he is on medication for a mental illness, but there is no way he will admit to the voices. The ones that threaten to kill the family if he doesn't do as they say.

It is while Carol and her father are weeding the veggie garden that he tells her that it was a mixed blessing when Robert moved out and found his own place. It gave them peace but it also left them worrying that he would not get help when he needed it most. They worried that no-one would be there when he rolled himself up into a ball, covered his ears, and rocked backwards and forwards for hours screaming 'no no no'.

Carol and Frank keep weeding the garden in silence after that. Each locked in their own thought cages. Focusing all their attention on Robert had drawn him to them. He arrives that same night. Out of the blue. Looking like he needs a good scrub and a feed.

Grateful to feel useful, Carol cooks up his favourite pasta dish. Long after their dad has gone to bed, they stay up chatting, with Carol doing most of the chatting, rabbiting on about her new job, her kids, and how she is filling in her time there.

'How about you?' she finally asks.

'I've done that many gardens,' he says, turning his head to the veggie garden now well hidden in the dark.

'Every time I rent a house I get stuck into the garden.'

They sit with that for a while.

'Are you interested in hearing about that?' he asks.

'Of course.'

'Well I've discovered biodynamics, mainly from the web.'

'Go on.'

'I've been making my own preps. You have to dilute them by about a million, and stir them clockwise and counter-clockwise for hours, and then spread it all around with a switch from a special tree. It sounds weird, doesn't it, but the citrus trees are loaded with huge bright coloured fruit and the veggies taste like, well, real veggies.'

Carol reaches for her phone.

'Would you believe Brook is into biodynamics. I'll send you her number. Ring her, she would love to know that there is someone else in the family who's into all of that.'

'Wonder if there is a good gardener gene in our family.'

'Bound to be,' she agrees.

Then he says, 'Dad's been telling you, hasn't he. Dad's been telling you about how I get sick and the trouble I've been in.'

And she has to say, 'Yes, he has.' She wants to say, 'But it doesn't make any difference', but she can't because it does make a difference. She wants to ask, 'Do you want to tell me about any of that?' but she doesn't because she is afraid of what he might tell her. She wants to say, 'It will be OK, you know,' but she knows very well it is not OK, and it has not been OK for a long long time, and it will never be OK.

Robert breaks the silence. 'It's OK Sis. We don't have to talk about it now. I'll come back to see you and Dad, and we might talk about it then. Anyway, I wouldn't know where to start.'

He stands up slowly. 'Have you noticed, Sis, the trees around here are behaving oddly for summer?'

'Yes. It was happening around the house in Sydney too.'

'Everyone talks about how lucky we are with day after day of sunshine. But it's the drought that in places like this, we don't even call a drought. The trees know it is a drought. Even the native ones are shedding leaves.'

He paces. She watches him.

'The trees can tell us so much if you know how to read them.'

'Yes.'

'The grass is too brittle here. I'll have to leave here. I need to go home.'

She stands up and puts her arms out to him. He steps forward and allows her to wrap her arms around him tight.

Then he turns and walks into the house with a 'G'night.'

She walks down the road, to her new little home. She doesn't feel as if she is crying but the tears keep rolling down her face.

Carol stays up late, writing Robert into her notes, putting in the few good bits she can remember, as well as the sadness of his mental illness. She thinks of her dad, finally unburdening himself and wondering if it is his way of saying that he does not want to do it all by himself any longer. Of saying that the pattern can now be broken.

'So, where from here?' she asks herself. 'How do you start to break the pattern?'

She writes herself a big sign, to phone Andrew and Jennifer.

She tells herself that from tonight, Robert is every-one's business.

The sensible Carol chimes in, 'Idiot. How can they help? They are not even here.'

'OK,' she tells herself, 'at least they can know about it.'

Carol has another restless night, waking up from dreams about the strange behaviours of trees turning bare when they didn't take their medication.

ELEVEN

Carol sees the black car pull into the drive-way. She pulls back from the window, where she has been watching for its arrival, failing to divert herself with emails, new novel, or a mindfulness podcast.

He unfolds his long body as he lets himself out of the driver's seat. He stands tall. She can't help noticing how tall as he stretches his arms over his head, bending down from the waist and lifting up again. Spot of lower spine trouble there, she says to herself. Can't take sitting in the car for too long. She expects him to unload his things, unlock his house, and settle in a bit, like he has before, but he doesn't. He looks straight at the cabin, gives a big smile and a wave, and comes straight to her open door.

A big bear hug. She hangs in there as long as he is willing. He pulls back, looks straight at her face and says, 'I need a beer in the beer garden overlooking the beach. I need a good feed of fish and chips. And then we can talk about tonight.'

'Let's do the beer and the fish and chips and take it from there.'

'Yep. OK with you if we walk?'

'Sure,' she says.

She steals a few glances sideways wondering who this man is. She sees a large grown up version of a teenage Turner boy, now probably in his mid fifties, with an open smiling face and a confidence she can see in his very stride as they start walking along the beach, to the next beach and the next.

In her nervousness, she is doing most of the talking. She is telling him how it is for her, down here, on the coast, with no friends, none of her regular patients, with her kids off doing their own things and with her siblings either far away and useless or close to home and mad. She is telling him about being the hub of this family wheel which she is trying to somehow control while it spins round and round. She tells him she is not even sure how much her dad needs her but she gets stuck into thinking she's indispensable, but that's quite stupid, isn't it, because after all, no-one is really indispensable, are they?

Jack has been matching his pace to hers as she speeds up and slows down. He's taking it all in.

'Well perhaps some are. Like for some very needy child. Or some very needy adult. Sometimes there is no other option, and then some people do become the unwilling indispensables.'

Carol stops.

He turns to her.

'But sometimes,' he says, 'there is also collusion.'

'Collusion?'

'Yes. The ones who think they are indispensable when they are not collude by doing it all.'

'Well that's pretty profound.' Carol catches herself just in time. She does not add 'for a lawyer.'

She is not telling him about the dark stuff she's learning about. She's not telling him about Robert or that he has just visited and she doesn't know if he got home alright.

They keep walking. Around the headland, hopping over rocks, reaching the second beach. Carol is enjoying the silence. She is grateful he doesn't have to fill it with his own family rave. She is starting to relax into this beautiful day.

'Don't you just love this warm autumn weather,' she says out loud. 'Look how the late afternoon sun is sparkling on the water.'

Jack comes out of his own reverie. 'It's called drought.'

Dammit, she thinks to herself. Of course it is.

They keep walking the length of the next beach on the hard sand, where the waves are only ankle deep, and where they have to race up the soft sand to avoid the occasional big crashing wave. They get to the pub with the beer garden overlooking the sea, eat fish and chips and leave the limp salad. They are talking non-stop now, not a word about families. Not a word about the drought.

He has just come back from three weeks walking in Nepal and stayed a few extra weeks in a village mostly playing ball games with the kids. He has found an ethical travel agency where you can do that sort of thing. Time for you first, and then volunteer time that they arrange for you according to your likes and skills. He has taught kids swimming in Burma, and soccer in the hills in Thailand. He wants to know what she could do.

Carol stops to think about that one. Perhaps set up a vege-table garden. Perhaps knitting. How domestic. No. How about swimming. 'I have taught kids that.' He says she seem to have forgotten she is a physiotherapist and would be very much in demand. He says perhaps they could find a trip they would like to both go on. How about Cuba? Cuba sounds great to Carol. Cuba sounds just far enough away.

She asks him how he got into volunteering overseas and he says it was from a friend.

Silence. But she is curious. 'Well, how come?'

'A woman I knew,' he says. 'Actually, a woman I was going out with.' Silence. 'A long time ago.' Silence. 'We travelled together quite a bit, but then she ended up staying in Asia. I think she's running an outpost hospital in Cambodia now.' Silence.

'It was quite a blow to my ego that she settled for that kind of life instead of settling down with me.'

'Yes,' Carol agrees. 'I guess it was.'

There was so much more she wants to ask him. All in good time, she cautions herself. Just don't rush him.

Carol can't help looking at his body. Still in pretty good shape. Some thickening about the waist. Hair a bit thin on top. But his attentive eye contact is unnerving her. And when he smiles, which is often, his eyes almost disappear into the crinkles. And when he laughs it comes from deep belly down. For the first time in a long time Carol is gazing at the man she knows she will be making love with that night. And she knows that the way he has been looking, listening, leaning forward across the table, he is feeling exactly the same way.

They walk back along the beach in the twilight. She unlocks the cabin door and they walk inside like it is something they do every day.

She lights the candles that have lived neglected in their pretty holders on the shelves. She turns back the bed-cover and throws back the doona. She goes to show him the tiny bathroom and then remembers, of course, he knows exactly where it is.

He completes a round of the cabin in five large step, and looks at the bed saying 'It's been a while,' just as she starts saying 'It's been a while' and they both start laughing.

She forgets about the music she had put handy just in case. She forgets about her own body that has thickened over the past few years. She forgets about her breasts, sagging from breastfeeding too long.

Tonight Carol feels beautiful as she slowly peels off her jeans and best cotton top, slips off her bra and steps out of her panties. Tonight she feels adolescently young and womanly mature. Tonight she is looking at his naked body and wanting it to last forever.

They are both hungry for it. They fiercely grip each other tight. She explodes just before he does. She feels him pumping his semen deep inside her. They stay holding each other. Lying back on the pillows they turn to look at each other, holding eye contact, smiling, wordless, resting, knowing there is plenty more night and there is lots more love to be making.

They sleep like spoons together, her mind rambling through gratitude for her early menopause and putting her faith in him being free of nasty diseases.

The weekend flies. Swimming in the sea. Good food. Junk food. Good wine. Talking. Walking. And sex, beautiful sex. First thing in the morning. Between sleeps at night.

And then he is gone.

Once she said to him, 'Do you know what my dad said about you?'

'Please tell.'

She puts on Frank's voice. 'You want to watch out for yourself, Girlie, with that Turner boy.'

'Is that all he said?'

'No. Not married and too good looking for his own good.'

'Quite right, you should watch out for yourself. Like next weekend. Are you OK about me coming down next weekend?'

Carol laughs. 'I don't know how Dad knew that we were going to spend the weekend together. I certainly didn't tell him.'

'Small town. They put two and two together and get sixteen. But it's nice to know your dad's looking out for you. He must care about you such a lot.'

And she thinks. Yes, he must.

But at the end of the weekend she says to him that it was funny that they spent the whole time in her little cabin when there was a whole house about five metres away. And he says that the cabin felt perfect. It felt like a special place for him. He said that the oldest kids in the family got the cabin, so he never got the chance. He gives her the key to the house, and says she can go in anytime, and then she will understand why he likes the cabin so much.

She doesn't think much about this, but one day, after the rain finally came and pelted down for days, she's tempted to look at another space, a different four walls, a hall perhaps, or a real kitchen where you do more than pivot on one foot to reach everything.

Not such a good idea. This furniture, the curtains, rugs, and everything are just as she remembers it as a child. It's a museum piece. A photo of itself from forty years ago. She moves around it slowly. She opens the clunky wooden cupboard doors in the kitchen and sees old aluminium saucepans, an electric Sunbeam fry-pan, a wooden rolling pin and rusty biscuit cut-out shapes of Christmas trees and Easter rabbits. She sees knives with bone handles, a table with a red marbled Formica top and stainless steel legs splayed out at a crazy angle.

Carol walks into the dark living room and pushes back the heavy curtains. She runs her hand over the built-in radio/record player and notices the 78s lined up in their faded paper covers.

It smells musty. Stale. It smells of a house locked up and neglected. It smells of dampness imprinted in its floor and in its walls. Suddenly she needs to get out. She quickly locks the door and runs back to her blessed cabin.

She wants to phone Jack straight away and ask him what on earth that museum was doing in her front yard. She knew he stayed there from time to time. He brought his mates there. Did they grow fungus on their skin? Did they dress up and pretend they lived in a bygone time? Or did they just drink their beer, eat takeaways and play darts in between their swims and their kayaking and not notice too much at all.

The phone rings. It's Jack.

'Hi.'

'You all right?' he says. 'You sound a bit stressed.'

'I've just been in the house. I got a bit of a shock,' she says. 'I didn't expect it to be like that.'

'Oh,' he says.

'Yeah, like nothing's changed. Nothing updated. Nothing thrown out. Nothing new. It's all like it was when we were kids. I've never seen a house where nothing gets changed.'

'Well,' he says and she can hear his voice coming from a different place. 'Well,' he goes on, 'you know, it will all go, one day soon or not so soon. All these houses will just go. The sea is getting warmer, the cyclonic activity is coming further and further south, the sea surges are getting bigger and the high tides higher.'

He pauses for breath while Carol holds hers in.

'When the dunes are flattened by the sea surges, the houses still standing will be flattened by the big tides. And if the water doesn't come into the houses from the sea first, then it will be the water racing down the escarpment in the big rains.'

Carol waits, wanting to ask 'Oh, is that all?' But it wasn't.

'Or it might be the river breaking its banks and the water coming sideways. Inwards, downwards or sideways doesn't really matter. They will all be gone.'

He stops for breath.

'Jack, I ….'

'So why would anyone update anything that is so bloody temporary?'

He rings off.

Carol feels cold. The wind is blowing hard on the cabin. It feels cold and damp inside.

She flops down on the bed and covers herself with the doona. She lets the thoughts in, slowly, one by one. This side of Jack, well, she hadn't predicted that. She wonders about his certainty that all the houses are doomed. But she wonders about Jack. What else?

The phone rings.

It's him.

'I'm sorry. I didn't mean to upset you just now. But it's just how things are.'

'It's OK.' She lies. 'Thanks for ringing back. It's OK. It's the reality most of us don't want to face.'

'We'll talk more about it next weekend. Still OK if I come down?'

'Yes, of course. I really want you to.'

'Do you?'

'Sure.'

'Bye then.'

'Bye.'

But Carol isn't sure she will be ready for the next weekend. She reaches for her laptop. She begins her search. She needs to know the facts, how bad will it get and how soon. She finds maps for worst case scenario flooding on the South Coast. She finds predictions of sea rise with rising temperatures, and rising temperatures with rising carbon dioxide content in the air. She sees predictions of cyclones becoming more common further south. How far south? It all depends on factors that all depend on other factors and then she hasn't even factored in the melting of the ice caps and the effects of the reduced snow fields. What does that mean? She still doesn't know if Jack is way off, losing it, catastrophising, or just plain able to face the truth that no-one else is facing.

Her phone rings.

'Hi Mum.'

'Brook. Hullo love. How's my girl?'

'Well things are a bit difficult at the moment. Have you got a minute? Are you in the middle of something important?'

As if, she thinks. 'Take your time, love. What is it?'

'Mum, we're thinking of moving over to the coast.'

Carol does not need this phone call. Not just now. Not when her head is full of images of the water coming in, coming down, coming across, all at the same time, and all these lovely beach houses, and all the new schmick concrete mansions that are springing up with their three car garages, all smashed to pieces with cyclonic tides. And this little cabin, floating out to sea like a houseboat, bobbing along taking in water and slowly sinking into the bay.

'Yes? Why now? What's this about?'

'Mum. Todd and I are seriously thinking we might start a family soon.'

'Yes. That's great!'

'But we have to move away first. It's a bummer as we both have good jobs here, and it is hard enough to find work outside Sydney and we don't want to live in the city. We don't want to bring up kids in the parts of the city we could afford to live.'

'Tell me why you have to move then. I thought you were pretty settled. It's a lovely country town, and you seem to have friends, and a house and jobs and what else do you need?'

'It's the coal trains that go through here – right near the farm and then through the town. At first I didn't think so much about them especially when we moved out to the farm. Did I tell you I manage it now? And Todd is doing a great job as the environmental officer at the mine. So we weren't thinking so much about the coal trains.'

'What coal trains?'

'From the mine of course. They snake their way through this little town, close to the back of the shops, alongside the sports ground, behind the school, and over the river where the breeze is often blowing back into town. Each train is a kilometre long.'

'Well, aren't they covered?' she asks.

'No. Only coal trucks have to cover their load. It's second rate, this coal Mum. It has a lot of fine dust particles. There is black dust everywhere. It's getting worse with more and more coal trains since the mine expansion. Even out here, we see it on our car every morning. The black dust sticks on our windows. It is in the air. We are breathing dust particles at a level that no city in Europe would tolerate.'

Carol can hear the panic in Brook's voice like when she was little, and frightened of the big storms up north. When the lightning used to light up their little house like it was day. When the claps of thunder made them all jump. And when the rain came down so loud on the tin roof they couldn't even hear the TV or the phone ringing.

'So, love,' she says trying to hose down Brook's panic, 'moving does sound like a good idea. I guess you and Todd need some time to plan this. Getting new jobs. Somewhere you can afford the rents, or perhaps to buy. But the coast is getting really expensive. You wouldn't believe the prices down here.'

'I want to move now, Mum. I want to get away. We drink that coal dust in the water we catch off our roof. We eat it when it lands on the farm vegetables that are supposed to be biodynamic. How biodynamic is coal dust? We take it in with every breath.'

'Hey, slow down love. Just tell me, what do you need to move? What do you need most right now?'

Her very quiet voice comes through almost at a whisper.

'Do you think we could come down and stay with Granddad for a few weeks? I hardly know him, but Todd and I could help look after him. We could be useful. We could suss out the job market down there. We could spend some time with you.'

Carol stops to take in that her strong independent daughter is reverting to her frightened little girl.

'Sure, love. I'll ask Granddad tomorrow.'

They hang up. Carol does not add that Brook's granddad doesn't need yet another couple of people looking after him. Well, not now.

Carol gives herself a few moments. My girl. My poor baby girl.

She reaches for her laptop. She can remember reading some articles about coal dust containing heavy metals, and is determined to find out just what her girl was breathing and drinking in along with the coal dust. But where was the research information from Australian studies? Surely they, the government, the health department, universities or whoever had done studies on the effects of heavy metals from coal trains and from open cut mines on the health of pregnant women and babies, or even just people. But no. There are studies from USA and Turkey and Russia but not from here. She finds plenty on the damning health effects of tiny dust particles, Increased heart and lung diseases, cancers, high blood pressure and kidney disease.

She gives up her search and tells herself that she doesn't know much but she knows enough to want to get Brook out of there long before she gets pregnant.

Carol throws on her long wind jacket, puts the phone in her pocket and heads out for a walk along the beach. In the dark, she can just make out the white water caps that are riding the waves all across the bay. The wind is stirring up the dry sand into little eddies. She can just see enough to walk.

The two phone calls have left her edgy. She wonders if it is just these two or if the whole world is going mad. On a sudden impulse she stops, walks over to the dune, puts her back to the wind and dials Jonah.

'Hi Jonah. It's me.'

'Yeah. Hi Mum. Are you OK?'

'Yes of course, I just had an urge to phone you to see if you are OK.'

'Sure. Why the urge?'

Good question. They didn't talk much, except when they had something they really wanted to discuss and then they could go on for ages.

'Oh, I don't know. Brook is a bit strung out about there being more and more coal mining near her, and about the dust from the coal trains that run near the farm.'

'Yeah, well she has every reason to be strung out about that. It's crazy Mum. Country is supposed to be where there is fresh air and pure water, but it's not like that anymore. At least not up where she is. She should get out.'

'Yes, she and Todd want to come down here and take a bit of time out to decide where to move to next. But tell me what's going on for you now.'

Carol needs him to be alright. She needs someone to be alright and she can usually rely on Jonah.

'Mum, I'm fine. Really. But I'm glad you rang. I wanted to talk to you about a job offer I've had in Melbourne. It's with a big international action group. It's running campaigns using social media.'

'I thought you were happy working locally and living away from the big city.'

'It's over here for the native timber. People just want jobs and there is work in the timber mills. There's no support for conservation any more.'

'Sounds like you are ready for a change.'

'They head-hunted me, Mum. I've never been head hunted before. And its kind of flattering to be wanted.'

'Sounds good love.'

'Yeah. Hey I sort of have to go. Haley's just serving up dinner, but it's good to hear from you, Mum. Don't worry about Brook. She and Todd will work it out.'

'Bye then.'

Haley? Carol wonders. Who the hell is Haley? And what is she doing serving up dinner for my boy at 10 o'clock at night?

Carol turns back to walk home. Tomorrow is a work day. Patients, case plans, objectives, small gains, team meetings, a small cog in a well oiled wheel. How normal. Why can't families be that simple? And relationships, too?

※ ※ ※

The next night, Carol and her dad are sitting on the verandah, watching the rain pelt down. She puts it to him. She asks him if Brook and Todd could come and stay for a while and his answer put a smile on her face. Sometimes she just loves him to bits.

'No way, Girlie,' he says. 'No way do I want to share my home with those two younguns. But I'll ask around. There is sure to be another cabin like yours they could afford to move into. It would be fun to have them down here for a while, eh. Does the boy fish?'

Walking home, she calls Brook with the news and finds out that yes, the boy does fish.

Carol feels calmer now with an inner warmth about her lovely girl coming back into her life again. Despite Jack's fears, she feels this place, this place of her childhood holidays, is safe for all of them.

She smiles as she can see, on this very beach, the four of them as kids, playing games on this sand, catching waves on a good surf day on their boogie boards, eating barbequed sausages in buns with tomato sauce, their parents letting them roam wild, knowing Jennifer was there, with Andrew's puffer in her pocket and that she would herd them back home before dark.

TWELVE

Jack puts the phone down. He sits, head in hands, staring at his big feet.

'Big bloody mouth,' he mutters to himself. 'I fucked it again. Another fuck up.'

He puts on his running shoes, grabs a hat, thrusts a front door key and his phone into his back pocket and heads out the door.

He runs. Down the hill to the sea. South along the beach. He keeps running along the coastal path linking the beaches till he is totally out of breath and his legs are cramping.

He takes a long drink from the beach bubbler and flops down on the grass, closing his eyes and letting his body come back to nearly normal.

And then he can think.

He picks at an old thread and begins to tease at it. It's been counselled to death, this thread. Yes, it started with her, back then, when he thought he could have everything. Her, his career, a house, a family, the lot. Except she didn't want a house or a family or the lot. He never was able to dispel her fears about not having healthy normal children. She said her family had given birth to enough mad people and she didn't need to add a few more. For the first time in his life he realised he could not have everything he wanted. His perfect future crashed.

'So why,' he asks himself, 'am I going over this now? Why do I go over this every time I fuck up?'

He pictures Carol. He thinks about the long summer holidays down the coast as a child, and he can just remember her as that freckle-faced little kid from the family his mother used to sigh about with a 'there's something not quite right about that family'. But he and his brothers played with them when they needed the numbers for cricket or when the little kids hung around looking like they wanted someone big to play with.

And he pictures her now. There is a strong purposefulness about her. He likes the way she's put her life on hold to come down to be near her father for a while. He's getting fascinated that her family can be so complex. Was his mother right all those years ago?

His family seems so ordinary by comparison. His hard-working plumber dad and teacher mum setting firm limits on their four boys who played good rugby and did OK at school work. They're still all OK. Well, mostly he's OK. He's still close to all three of them. He's the favourite uncle to all of their kids.

He thinks about how the years had almost flashed by, with his career and his travels and his few long and failed relationships, and he really doesn't want to go there any more about long and failed relationships because that too has been well and truly done over one way or another.

Carol. He can see her at the door of the cabin, with the sun on her hair, and her eyes lighting up at the sight of him, and her hungry body, and her effortless chatter, drawing him into her world like it is somewhere he naturally belonged.

'I want to belong in your world,' he says out loud. 'I'm so over mine.'

And then the dreadful realisation creeps in once more, 'I've fucked up.'

He draws a deep breath. His old logic kicks in.

First define the problem.

How could I be so stupid blabbing about the coastal thing?

No, this is not the problem.

Perhaps I'm catastrophising a bit.

This is not the problem.

OK. I have put my new relationship at risk.

Yes. So?

At worst she thinks I'm a crackpot and she will gently but firmly break it off next weekend. At best she thinks I am being a bit over-dramatic but will hang in there to see what else I have to offer.

'And then,' he thinks, 'there is everything in between.'

So?

Go gently with her and you might also tell her how you are feeling about her.

OK.

It is now quite dark. Jack heaves himself up and walks over to the line of closed cafés. He rings for a taxi to take him home.

THIRTEEN

Andrew wakes to the sound of his phone. He reaches across to the bed-side table and resists the urge to leave it when Carol's name comes up on the screen.

'Hi Carol.'

'Hi, is this too early in the morning for you?'

'No, it's all good. Christopher and Paul are both still asleep? So how is the south coast treating you?'

'Oh, it is still so beautiful. I'm happy. I see quite a bit of Dad, I've got work, and I might have the beginnings of a romance thing happening.'

She immediately regrets this last bit.

'So how's Dad?'

'He's managing really well. He goes quiet at times and I know he misses Mum heaps, but he's fishing with old friends. Guess what, he goes ballroom dancing at the RSL and is in great demand. But I suppose you see a bit of him when he and Christopher are skyping.'

'Fat chance. I'm not even allowed in the room!'

'And how's my nephew? I really miss being able to get to know him. You all seem so far away.'

'He's nearly as tall as Lisa, but I can still beat him in tennis.'

'Hey, Andrew, I want to talk about Robert.'

'Sorry, but I don't.'

'What do you mean you don't?'

'Carol, it's not difficult to understand. It is just a 'No'. I don't want to talk about Robert.'

'Well I do. Dad's getting old. Mum's not around any more. And Robert gets sick and needs help. It's a family problem.'

'Is Dad saying he can't cope with it?'

'No, of course not. As if he would.'

'Is Dad saying he can't cope generally?'

'Of course not.'

'Well, how do you know he is getting too old to cope?'

'Because I am here, and you, you are not.'

'Yes, you are there. But does Dad need you to be there?'

'He seems to like it. And anyway, we couldn't all abandon him with Mum dying and all.'

'True. Yes. And I happen to live half way across the world. Exactly what do you think I can do about Robert?'

'At least listen!'

'Listen? How about you listen. Carol, there is no way you could understand what it was like for me, as a male, to be growing up in the shadow of the great and wonderful hero, with him being everything Dad wanted in a son, and me, playing inside with Lego all weekend with an asthma wheezing chest. And him getting all those prizes on speech day for hero subjects like maths and science when all I could manage was the music prize that no-one cared about anyway.'

Carol does not know what to do with this. She hears a different voice.

'Hi Carol. Paul here. How about we leave it now. I don't think this is really getting anywhere.'

'Oh, Paul. I just want him to know what's going on.'

'Yes. I understand. But he wants to be left out. Sorry. He just wants out. OK?'

'That's not OK. Goodbye.'

Carol puts the phone down. She paces up and down the small length of the cabin, muttering 'It's not OK. It's such a cop out. How does he think he can just cut himself off from his own brother?'

She desperately wants to phone someone, talk to someone who would understand. And dammit. She cannot think of a single soul.

※ ※ ※

An overwhelming sadness envelops Andrew as he turns to Paul.

'Thanks mate,' he says. 'I am so sorry you had to wake up to that.'

Andrew lies back on the pillows. He thinks about all the times he did wish that Robert would fall off his perch, fail at something, yes, and even get a disease, but, he has to admit to himself, he hadn't actually thought of him becoming psychotic, which was just as well in a way, because as Mum so often said to them, 'You have to be careful what you wish for.'

He also feels sad about Carol. It should have been light, friendly, swapping stories of what they had been up to since his visit back home. Even touching perhaps on how they were dealing with their mum's death. But not this. Not ringing with a big unrealistic expectation that centres on her needs to involve him in her control plan. But then he stops himself. That bit's not fair. If there is any controller in the family it is Jennifer. Jennifer who was always there and keeping it all together, that is, as long as you did it her way.

'We can talk about this tonight if you want,' says Paul, starting his morning routine of getting up, showering and getting breakfast while Andrew coaxes Christopher out of bed.

※ ※ ※

Carol sets off on her half hour drive for her evening shift at the rehabilitation centre. She is still muttering. 'Selfish little prick. Cowardly little runaway. Fucking Andrew.'

As she turns out of the village along the narrow road leading inland to the highway, she puts it to the absent Andrew that if he wants to be left out of the whole family business, then how about he keeps his own theories to himself about who needs who most.

A sharp tooting makes her look in her rear mirror to see a truck closing the distance between them. She looks down seeing with horror that she has been crawling at about 40 k per hour in an 80 zone, and pulls over to the side of the road. As the truck roars past she notices it is carrying logs and wonders whereabouts they could be felling timber so close to the coast. Then she remembers the stickers plastered on the back of her car. Yes, there is the old 'Keep your hands off native forests.' She gives thanks that she wasn't run off the road, like some of her friends up north have been.

'OK,' she says to herself, 'calm down. Take a few minutes to finish thinking about this, and then, stupid, get yourself to work in one piece.'

Try as she might she cannot block out her conversation with Andrew. She hears his voice, 'Is Dad saying he can't cope with Robert?' She answers herself. Of course he's not. And anyway, would he say if he wasn't coping? Another thought creeps in. How about if he had made a promise to their mother to look after Robert when he was in trouble? What if, now there is no Gabby, Frank feels he should deal with it himself?

She lets out a big sigh. No. Dad won't live forever. We should all know about Robert and how his illness comes out. And anyway, it's not that simple. It's not about Dad needing me or not needing me. It's about wanting. I want to be spending some time with him, and he wants me there to hear his story. So there, Andrew.

And she drives off.

FOURTEEN

Carol gets herself a cup of tea, sits up on the double bed against a pile of pillows and braces herself to phone Jennifer.

But it is John who answers.

'Hi John, is Jennifer around?'

'Yeah, oh hi, yeah, she's just finishing off her batch of fig jam for the show. Can she call back in half?'

'Sure.'

'Anyway how are you, John?'

'Oh, thanks for asking, fine.'

'And how are the twins doing at school?'

'Oh, fine.'

'Oh, that's good.'

'Yes.'

'OK, goodbye. Can you remind Jennifer to phone back then?'

'Sure, goodbye.'

Carol rings off. She never really could work John out. Am I alright? Well, thanks for asking John. Actually mostly I am, but sometimes I do wonder what I am doing down here, so far away from my home and my friends. And how are my kids? Well thanks for asking, John. Both are a bit unsettled at the moment, both looking at moving, both looking at changing their jobs. Brook especially is having a hard time living so close to an open cut mine.

She reminds herself to ask Jennifer about herself a bit before getting onto Robert. Especially about the foal. It is difficult to put herself into a sister space, because Carol never did feel much like Jennifer's sister. They didn't play together. They didn't swap clothes.

Carol remembers two of her close friends at school who had big sisters, and they seemed more like her big sisters than Jennifer ever was. From them she learnt about mascara and eye-liner and how to walk in high heeled shoes. But then, Carol thinks to herself, Jennifer wasn't into make-up or high shoes herself. She cared more about riding boots and jodhpurs for pony club.

The shrill ring of her phone brings Carol back to the now.

'Hi Jennifer, thanks for calling back.'

'Hi.'

'How did the grape jam turn out?'

'It's fig.'

'Oh, yeah, well how is it?'

'I'm not sure. I like to cook it a bit longer so it tastes a bit caramelly, but the judges like it to be a lighter colour so I might miss out this year.'

'It must be hard to weigh up what you want in a jam and what the judges want.'

'Yes it is. I like getting even a second or third prize but then we are the ones who eat it.'

'Can you take a few jars out a bit early for the show and then let the rest cook a bit longer?'

'That's not such a stupid idea.'

Carol sighs with relief that she is not totally stupid about jam. 'John tells me the twins are doing well at school.'

'Yes, as long as they are getting good grades, he thinks they're alright, but I'm a bit worried about Janet. I think she's flirting with the notion of being anorexic. I've asked John Junior about her, but of course he hasn't noticed anything. The school says there is nothing to worry about – all girls that age don't like being even the slightest bit fat, but Janet was hardly fat, she was just a good strong healthy girl.'

'Did you notice anything when she was home last holidays?'

'Well I don't get to see her that often. She went to her friend Sally's place last holidays even though I suggested to her that Sally could come here, but Sally has a pool and a big brother and I think they thought summer would be pretty dull here.'

'Are you planning to visit Janet and John Junior soon?'

Jennifer takes a deep breath.

'I just have. I went over earlier this week.'

'Oh, that's good.'

'No, it's not good at all. We couldn't really afford the petrol. We owe thousands on the school fees. They will have to leave at the end of the term. No more credit.'

Carol can hear the tension rising in her sister's voice.

'That's tough.'

Carol waits for Jennifer to explain a bit more about this. But instead, her big sister changes the subject.

'How's Dad going?' she asks

'He's doing really well. He seems to have started a new phase of his life without Mum. He keeps busy enough. You know how he likes to plan his time. Well he's doing just that, but doing different things now that he is on his own. We go walking once a week but I try not to get in his way or go there too much.'

'So you don't spend that much time with him then?'

'Not really. I'm working part time and I like to keep fit.'

'What else are you doing?'

Guilt. Deficient. Slack. Carol has nothing to offer. She pictures Jennifer with her busy nursing job, the work she has to do on the farm, singing with her band at the club, a husband who is depressed with the drought, a daughter who is possibly turning anorexic, and still finding time to make jam.

She lamely offers 'I guess it's taken a bit of time to settle in here,' as she looks around at the tiny cabin that needs about an hour's housework a week.

'Hey, Jen. I want to talk to you about Robert.'

'Why, isn't he taking his medication?'

'Well, I am not sure about that. I've only seen him once since I moved down and he seemed pretty medicated then, but you know, Dad's getting older and it's not fair that he should carry all of that. We should at least be thinking about supporting Robert so that he knows we all care about him too and are there for him when he needs it.'

'Look, Carol.'

Carol braces herself.

'Caring about him and being there for him are very different. Yes, of course I care about him. But seriously I am not there for him. I think it's great that you are there to take some of the pressure off Dad. After all, you were always the one that got on best with Robert.'

Carol sits there. Silent. No answers and one hundred answers flood into her brain. She can feel her sister prickle through the silence. She changes tack.

'Jen, have you been talking with Andrew about this?'

'Yes, of course we talk. He told me you'd been onto him about the same thing. Honestly, Carol, give us a break. We didn't make him psychotic.'

'And do you think someone did?'

'No, of course not. Look it's sad and it shouldn't have happened, but get real. We both are just too far away and we both have such full lives just now. I know it's not what you want to hear, but it's just how it is.'

'OK.'

'Give my love to Dad, won't you.'

'Sure'

'Bye then.'

Carol puts down the phone, glad she forgot to ask about the stupid foal. She pours herself another glass of red wine. Two blanks. Two rejections. Two fucking selfish siblings that don't want to take any responsibility. No, two siblings that don't even want to hear about it. Right. So all that family history from Dad, perhaps they don't want to hear about that either. Perhaps they won't even be offered the chance to know.

Carol strips off her clothes and jumps into a hot shower, letting the water run over her head, calming her anger, washing it all away – shampoo, conditioner, soap, scrub.

'OK,' she says out loud, 'it's you and me, Robert.'

She dries herself off with hard strokes, picks up her phone and dials Jack's number.

'It's me. Carol. When is it again that you were thinking of coming down to do some work on the house?'

He laughs. He says how glad he is that she called. He says he is planning to come down the next weekend. He says he is coming by himself and will she have some spare time? He says he is looking forward to that.

＊ ＊ ＊

Jennifer hangs up and then, on sudden impulse she phones back. 'Hi Carol, it's me again. Sorry to bother you but there is stuff I didn't say before.'

'Mmm.'

'Carol, I hate to dump on you like this, but things have sort of got to crisis point out here and the bank manager is being difficult about our overdraft because, well, it keeps going up instead of down.'

Carol wonders if she is meant to be just listening to this or if there is something she is supposed to be offering. Like mortgaging her house.

Jennifer continues. 'John wants to hang onto the farm. He feels like he has failed and he has to prove that he can do it like the generations of his family before him, but of course he can't. Well I finally had to say it's this farm or me, and so now he is thinking of selling and moving down onto a small irrigation holding on the river. We could do more intensive farming on a much smaller scale, and the twins could go to the local school. But no-one wants to buy out here. The Crosswell place has been on the market for two years. We don't have two years.'

Jennifer pauses for breath.

'And then, of course, down on the river country there is the salt.'

'Yes of course, the salt.'

'Well there's still irrigated farmland that hasn't got salt, but of course it's more expensive.'

'How do you know more irrigation won't make it salty?'

'The farming families down here, they know about that stuff.'

'Oh, right.'

There is a silence, while Carol can feel Jennifer getting up courage for the next bit.

'Carol, do you know what is holding up Dad giving us our share of the house? He rang to tell me that we can have it and then a big nothing, and we really do need it to start paying off the bills. Like right now. It might lift John out of his depression. I've never seen him like this. I don't like leaving him to do my shifts at the hospital, especially at night. If we had a way out ....'

'Look I'm really sorry about all of that. Why don't you phone Dad and have a talk to him about it?'

'I don't want him to know I'm kind of desperate. He doesn't need that. I just thought you might have some idea as you're down there.'

'I think you need to ask him yourself. I'm sorry Jennifer, it's something I really do want to stay out of.'

Carol wants to feel smug. Look, I can be like you and Andrew. But she doesn't. She just feels plain sad.

✳ ✳ ✳

'Bloody hell,' Jennifer lets it out as a loud scream as she puts down the phone.

'After all I did for her.'

But there is no one to hear.

Suddenly the tiredness that has been building up hits Jennifer, and she stretches out on the lounge, worn out from the conversation but even more worn out from too many night shifts.

She flicks on the ABC rural radio station and tunes into a panel discussing the drought. She half hears about the increased hospital admissions they euphemistically call 'drought casualties'. They talk about 'the mother of all droughts'. They bring out the stats that show that no other generation of farmers had it that hard. They talk about the good old days before El Nino was even heard of.

Jennifer shuts it down. She doesn't need it. She sees it first-hand. Domestic violence is up. So are accidents with farm machinery. So are alcohol-related car accidents. Still, Jennifer is relieved to be getting more shifts. It puts food on the table. It buys petrol and diesel. But it does nothing for the overdraft.

Government drought relief was supposed to do that. 'Fat chance,' she says to herself.

She thinks about what is happening in the nearby town, too. The shopkeepers get no drought relief but their businesses are down to a trickle. One of the two cafés has shut. The rural supplies store has sacked half its workers. The dentist and his family has taken a much postponed trip to Asia. The bottle shop and the pub seem to be doing OK. And the hospital and community health are stretched beyond belief.

Jennifer is also pleased to be away from the farm more often. The days are bad enough with John planning a late autumn sowing, waiting for a weather forecast that has the word 'rain'. The nights are even worse now. She hears him banging about downstairs, and then going out for hours at a time.

Sometimes she asks, 'John, where do you go? What are you doing?'

And he just glares at her as if she is the one acting strangely and says 'Nowhere.' 'Nothing.' And sometimes, 'Nunna ya business.'

But it bugs her. She can't sleep until she hears the door creak and his footsteps leading him back to the bedroom.

'Shit.' Jennifer jumps up off the lounge. 'The foal.'

She quickly prepares the bottle of formula, puts on her boots and races out to the hay-shed.

The foal comes running to her. She puts the bottle into its mouth, and her arm around its warm velvet neck and feels the strong pull of its sucking reaching up her arm until it warms her heart.

She starts singing to him, 'I met my bright eyed little doll, down by the river side, down by the river side, down by the river side'.

She stands up in front of the foal, swaying her hips and singing to him, 'There's a track leading back …'

She stays till she's run through the whole program of next Saturday's night of 'Golden Oldies' at the Bowling Club.

Reluctantly, she kisses the foal and walks slowly back into the house.

That night, she prepares a special meal for her and John. She opens one of the last bottles of red wine, hoping it will keep John off the spirits for a while.

That night, after dinner, she hears the dogs barking as a four wheel drive pulls up outside.

That night she sees the neighbour's elderly father, Mr Cunningham, brush past her, calling out John's name, and marching straight to the formal living room they never use, and she sees John, heave himself out of the big chair in front of the TV, walk slowly into the living room and shut the door.

She hears angry shouting. John bellows that he would never pump water out of their shared creek. Not in a drought. No, not even for the horses. She hears Mr Cunningham shouting even louder that he knows what John did. They have evidence. John shouts back that he knows what that good for nothing son of Cunningham's has done. And the police know too.

The living room door suddenly swings open and John dashes out, and returns with two large glasses and the whisky decanter. The door slams shut again.

Jennifer finishes cleaning up the dinner things. She cannot move from the kitchen. She sits at the table, sipping the remains of the wine. She can no longer hear what is happening. She starts scrolling through her i-Pad for new jam recipes.

At last the two men emerge. They shake hands. Mr Cunningham says good night to her and lets himself out. She waits till she hears the four wheel drive take off, and then calls out to John, who is back in the TV armchair,

'What's going on? John, for Chrissake talk to me.'

She whips the TV controls from his hand and stands across from him. She stares with loathing at his slouch, his sprawling legs, his face red from the spirits. His smell.

'We reached a gentleman's agreement.'

'About what? What for?'

'Nunna ya business.' That phrase. Jennifer knows from bitter experience she will get nothing more from John that night or perhaps ever.

'Well, fuck you.'

As she turns to leave she looks down at the TV controls in her hand. She walks back into the kitchen, opens the fire door of the fuel stove, tosses the controls inside and shuts the door.

'Well, fuck you,' she shouts.

She goes outside, hoping the smell of burning plastic would be over by the time she has checked on the foal, hoping too that John will have fallen asleep in his chair.

As she feels her anger go down a few notches, she starts to think about what she has heard. She puts two and two together. So they have just sorted it out themselves, eh. Secret men's business. Ha.

She fixes up the couch with bedding for John. She goes upstairs to their bedroom and locks the door. She lies down, staring at the ceiling. Stealing water from a bordering creek. Lord knows what the Cunningham boy had been up to. Jennifer has a sudden urge to bring her children home, but not to this home, not to this father.

FIFTEEN

Robert is on the train to see Jennifer. He was sure she had said he should drop by any time. But now he is not so sure. He should have rung. He should have checked. Oh well, she is his sister after all.

The carriage is half empty and he has a window seat, food and drink in his backpack, a few clothes, and some money in his wallet that his dad has sent him. He has booked a rental motor bike in Wagga so he can be free to come and go as he pleases. He knows he will want to take off when the conversation keeps going round in circles about the costs of boarding school for the twins, the latest foal, the drought, and jam making. With a bike he can cross country to Canberra and meet up with some old mates from rehab. They might have a few parties. They might have something decent to smoke. He might pick up a girl. Or two.

Still, it will be good to reconnect with Jennifer. He is curious. He remembers, when they all met up after the funeral, realising that he hardly knew her anymore. He wonders how much of their mum was in Jennifer. It seems she might be better at nurturing her favourite animals rather than her kids. He wonders why they prefer to go to friends' places for the holidays. Is that normal for boarding school kids? He wants to suss it all out. Find out for himself who his big sister had become.

But Robert is edgy.

Robert knows only too well why he is edgy. He lives with premonitions that things are about to get out of control. And of course they do, sooner or later. Trouble is, not knowing how soon and how much later.

At last the train starts moving and the swish, swish, swish of the wheels on the tracks is soothing. Robert sits back, clasps his hands in front, nods imperceptibly to the rhythmic sound and lets his thoughts go wandering.

His father. He was always much closer to Dad, growing up. They would spend hours on the nearby football field, practising soccer strikes, and his dad playing goalie. And then walking home afterwards, they always had so much to talk about.

His mother. It was only after he started to get depressed that his mother really became important to him. It was like she knew at some level that what was going on for him was real, was scary, was important. He knew that she would have fought the world to get him whatever it was he needed to help him cope with the depths he was sinking into. Looking back, Robert realises it was all too hard for his dad, and while the love and support was still there, his dad could not hide his disappointment. He was totally baffled as to why this had happened, and their time together had another dimension to it. His dad became cautious. His dad retreated to the sidelines. His mum became the chief player.

And strangely it was his little sister Carol who instinctively followed their mother's lead. This boy-crazy, fashion-crazy, food-fad teenager would look intensely at her mother, knowing there was no point in asking how they were supposed to deal with Robert's new illness, tuning into her mum and seeing how it was done. She spent time being with Robert, sat with him in silence, fixing him his favourite smoothie, and sometimes she would take him outside where they would rake up autumn leaves into piles, pull weeds from the garden beds, turn the compost heap. Once they even went back to being kids sucking all the stink beetles off the citrus trees with mum's vacuum cleaner with their mum's ever vigilant face looking out the kitchen window. Meanwhile, Jennifer upstairs cramming for her exams, and Andrew upstairs in his room playing music.

Andrew upstairs in his room. Robert felt a pang of guilt about Andrew. What a sad little kid that one was. He could kick himself now at how selfish he had been as a big brother, so wrapped up in his sport, his good grades, his being captain of this and best at that, his dragging their Dad off and leaving Andrew in the female household. He knows he could have, should have done better. He could have, should have gone to the boring concerts where Andrew so excelled. He could have, should have rekindled his passion for Lego. He should at least have tried.

That chasm between them. He now longs to breach it. To start the healing. He doesn't blame Andrew at all. He understands that Andrew retreated like a little wounded animal from the huge family space Robert was taking up. History now. Sad and long gone.

Jennifer upstairs cramming for her exams. He never really understood that one. You didn't cram for exams. You picked out the most basic principles, rolled them around a bit till they made unforgettable sense and then everything fell into place from there. As long as it all made sense, you didn't have to cram anything. You knew that you could always work it out. It was weird how she had to make everything bigger and harder than it was. Like being the eldest. Sure, she must have been a great help with the three younger sibs, but Jesus, that stopped about the time that Andrew got out of nappies and went to preschool. Yet she still carried on like it was her job to sort out their tiffs and squabbles, to let them know when they got out of line, to remind them that their dad worked very hard and should come home to a peaceful home instead of a war zone, to get up them when the job roster on the fridge was neglected (was it ever not neglected?) and generally be a pain in the arse. Why didn't she just have fun like other kids, other teenagers, even other big sisters? Robert sighs. He just doesn't get it.

So why, he lets the question enter, is he on this train, on this day going to her farm, to spend time with her and him of the elastic sided boots, who never found a deodorant that worked, who complains that the traffic in Wagga is unbearable at peak hour (exactly what peak hour?) and whose greatest claim to fame is winning the fastest roping of a steer at the local rodeo.

And how about those kids of theirs? Do they exist? Why are they always away at boarding school? Doesn't Wagga have schools? He's their uncle and he can't even remember their names. Do they have their own names or are they just John Junior and little Jenny?

Robert must have slept for a while and when he opens his eyes he notices the light is fading in the late afternoon. He gazes out the window of the train, at the endless paddocks and distant hills. Every now and again he can see sheep crowded together, heads down, totally unaware that they are surrounded by packs of hungry lions who are gathering, plotting, waiting for the right moment to spring into action. And the naked savages with long knives hiding in the folds of the hills. Who are they after? The sheep? Surely not. The lions?

To Robert's horror the savages turn towards the train, brandishing their knives, running on their hairy bow-legs, on their bare feet, their hairy bodies glistening with sweat, their faces contorted showing their long sharp teeth. Their shouting changes to English. The ugly face nearest to the train window is taunting him. Bet ya couldn't slit Jennifer's long white throat.

Bet ya couldn't slit open the belly of that new foal. Bet ya couldn't string up the dogs. Bet ya couldn't run over both twins with ya motor bike.

Robert feels the absolute fear. He has to get rid of everything that identifies him. He pulls out his wallet and rips out the cards and driver's license. He puts them deep inside the rubbish bag that holds his half eaten lunch. He lurches down the train to the vacant toilet and stashes the lunch bag deep into the bin well below the damp paper towelling.

He makes his way back to his seat, checking all the while to see if THEY had got on the train yet. He shuts his eyes. When he opens them they are still there at the window. He can still hear them. He pushes up his sleeve and places his thumb on his eagle tattoo. No help. He wills them all to go away. No way. He breathes. But the air is fetid. It stinks.

The train pulls into Goulburn. He looks out the window and sees the country railway station with a few people waiting on the platform totally unaware of the impending danger. He grabs his bag, leaps off the train, crosses over to the other side of the station, sits down on an empty seat, puts his bag down between his knees, pulls his beanie over his head and crosses his arms firmly over his chest.

He rocks silently. He keeps rocking and starts keening softly on the empty station. Empty except for the station master who keeps an eye on Robert, till he thinks perhaps he should get help. Ambulance or police. He thinks Robert looks harmless and settles on ambulance.

✳ ✳ ✳

Carol feels her dad's unease when she goes to fetch him for their weekly walk. He says he hasn't been sleeping well. He says it's too hot and perhaps she should come back later. He says he doesn't remember if he has had lunch. He finally says he doesn't know why but he's worried about Robert. He says he will be alright and needs time to himself.

Feeling dismissed Carol heads down to the beach.

Now her body too feels encased in a deep unease. It starts with an ache in her stomach and radiates through her arms as they reach out to embrace her absent children, her father, her dead mother, her siblings, especially Robert. It spreads out from her body like a cloud that travels along this fragile coast line, inland into the polluted air and water of the coal fields splat in the middle of the farming food bowl, following the trickle of the once mighty inland rivers into the salty flatlands. She is in it and of it. She sees herself, Carol, standing inert and useless in the warming of the land and oceans, the melting of the ice caps and the decimation of too many species. She wonders if Jack's fear is contagious. She wonders if she has entered through his portal into his personal hell.

Carol feels an intense need to go north.

✳ ✳ ✳

Every day her dad asks Carol if she's been in contact with Robert. She tells him that she does try his mobile several times during the day and night. She tries telling him, well you know Robert, Dad. Most of the time we don't really know where he is and what he is doing. He often goes out of range for days, or just turns his phone off. So what's so different about now? He nods as if he is agreeing with her.

Carol has been taking late night calls from Jack. She is usually in bed, and he is out on his balcony looking at the night sky. When she tells him she is worried about Robert, he starts on a big rave about psychotics.

She asks him how he knows about this. And he says that she is not the only person to have a psychotic in the family.

'But you don't, do you?'

'No, but that woman I told you about who went to Cambodia. She had a brother like that as well as the odd aunt and grandfather who were also quite mad. And then there is the odd student. The ones who are so bright but drop out. And there were clients before that.'

He pulls himself up short to ask, 'Hey, do you want to talk about Robert?'

'I started picking up on Dad's worry about him, and now I'm having my own worries.'

'But you haven't heard anything, have you?'

'No.'

'Perhaps you need a distraction.'

✳ ✳ ✳

Carol gets a call at work.

'They've found him.'

'Oh Dad, that's great.'

'It's taken a whole week before he trusted anyone at the psych hospital enough to let them know his full name and about me and where I lived.'

'Is he OK?'

'He's OK enough to be discharged. When do you get off work? We'll go and get him, Girlie. We'll bring him home.'

Carol rushes through her last patient for the day, leaps into her car, picks up her dad and they start out.

'Look,' he says. 'I really appreciate this. I could do the drive myself, you know. I can manage him too. I've done so before and I can do it again.'

'I know that Dad. I just wanted to come along. Nothing much else to do. '

'OK.'

She looks across. These games they play. She's just as bad as he is. But how, she wonders, as she looks across at her father shrinking into the passenger seat, how do you tell him, you don't have to do it all by yourself anymore.

He looks ahead at the straight stretch of road.

'You could turn your indicator off now, Girlie.'

Carol squints into the setting sun that is so low her visor is little help and she has to shield her face with one hand and drive with the other. She looks across as her dad takes his hat off and pulls it down on her head. He is sitting up taller now to shield his own face. He has that old Dad look as he asks her gently, 'Ever been to one of these places, Girlie?'

'No.'

'Well then, there's a few things you ought to know.'

He starts with a warts and all description of harsh fluorescent lights, loud footsteps on the tiled floor, angry ravings from any meth patients that might be there, tea in paper cups with plastic spoons, high security doors to get in and to get out, long waits to see the psychiatrist, the social worker, the case worker, the nurse.

'If it's too much, you don't have to come in.'

'Thanks, Dad, but I think I'll be OK.'

They do wait and wait. They meet with the psychiatrist and the social worker. They call Robert in for a bit more discussion. And he is discharged with the nothing he arrived with, plus the week's supply of medication.

Robert plonks his exhausted, wasted body on the back seat of her car and immediately falls into a deep sleep that lasts all the way back to the coast. Carol drops them home, goes back to the cabin and crashes.

Early each morning she drops by to see how things are going. Each night too. Each day Robert starts looking stronger and amazingly her Dad looks strong too. He looks in charge. He looks like he has it all under control.

A week flies by and Robert wants to go home. He says he's fine now. But to Carol, he looks hollow. Like everything inside him has been emptied. All he wants is a lift to the private coach stop, a ticket and a few dollars, well a few hundred dollars. He wants to give the train a miss. Good one, they all agree.

'I need a few days,' her dad says. 'I need a few days to catch up on things.'

Gratefully, Carol says, 'Sure thing Dad,' thinking she could do with a few days herself. So she kisses him and gives him a hug, her fingers noticing the bones so close to the skin of his back. She feels such a surge of love for her dad that all she can manage is a 'See you later then.'

They both go into their own private recovery mode. Carol throws herself into work. She buys fish and chips on the way home. She stays up watching a stupid series. She eats blocks of dark almond chocolate. She takes Jack's calls. She wants to hear his voice. But not her own. She gives her dad a wide berth. Just a quick phone call at the end of the day. Yes, he's alright. Yes she's alright.

On her next day off from work she goes down early to have breakfast with her father. They move onto the swinging seat on the front verandah and sit there, looking at the still waters of the bay.

He says, 'I need to tell you about your mother because she told me, before she went, that she had meant to do it herself, but somehow she didn't manage to do that.'

Carol waits.

'I remember when Jennifer found Gabby's story and read it out to you all. I think Gabby meant you all to read it. It wasn't really about her love of skating, it was about the ice she said had formed around her heart. It was about her mother hugging her only the once. Only that time. It was about growing up in that family. Nobody hugged. Nobody even talked much. Nobody seemed to care about anyone else.'

He shifts in his seat.

'Her sister seemed to fit in fine. But Gabby never did. She wanted to belong to a family like her friends had. She wanted visitors in her house. She wanted to rip the closed curtains apart and let in the sunlight. She wanted laughter, and talk at the dinner table. She wanted someone to ask "How was school today?" We used to joke that she was the white sheep.'

'So how come, Dad? Who were they, her parents, and what was wrong with them?'

'I don't really know. Your mother didn't want anything more to do with them, after she left home. She just wanted to get on with the rest of her life. She used to say sometimes that her life started with leaving home at sixteen and moving in with the girls from the bank.'

'And with you, Dad. Her life must have really taken off when you two got together.'

'Yes, that's true. We did that for each other. We were adults, but in some ways we were children. Somehow we slowly grew up, emotionally, but it took time.'

He pauses.

She can see this is going to be the really hard part for him. So she waits while they both gaze out to sea.

'Sometimes she would seem to go into herself for weeks at a time. She would lose ground. I mean she seemed to go back to how she was. Feeling unloved. Feeling a failure. She said the ice was growing back.'

'So what did you do?'

'I didn't know what to do. And she was pretty stubborn, your mother. So we didn't do anything. We just coped somehow. Just the two of us. We put off having children. Needing to have enough money was our excuse. But of course it wasn't that at all.'

'Did you have friends who were having children.'

'Yes. From my work, all young couples. So, yes. The pressure came from them mostly. I think they were relieved when we finally got started.'

'Mmmm.'

'Your mother did get more confident with each child. I think it was hardest for Jennifer. She was still going in and out of her dark and fearful place. But when you came along, Girlie, you brought nothing but sunshine into her face. I don't want you to get a swelled head about this, but you were the most adorable baby that we had ever seen. And Andrew, well he had all three of you to fuss over him. Until the asthma hit. Then it was quite a different story.'

'How about her sister, Dad? Did they keep contact?'

'No. They didn't. I only saw her once and she was just like in the story. Beautiful, with wide intensely blue eyes, blond curls, and a very curvy body. She came, unexpectedly, to our house soon after their parents died in a car accident.'

'And Mum didn't even know that they had died?'

'No. But the sister only wanted to stay living in the family house, and to load onto Gabby all the stuff she didn't want.'

'How awful.'

'Yes. Gabby just agreed to everything so that she didn't have to face her sister anymore. So we said yes to the house and got a truck load of stuff we didn't need. But somehow Gabby did want the things that meant something to her mother.'

Carol slumps down with the guilt that she let all of those things go.

'That is such a sad story Dad. I don't remember her being any different from the other mums. Or you being different either from the dads. Except you two were so obviously in love, and stayed in love, and that has been such a wonderful thing to have, as a kid, growing up, when it seemed sometimes that every other kid's parents were going through a separation or trial separation or had done it all years before.'

But then she remembers about their bedroom. She doesn't know whether to bring it up, or how to. Or if it was fair to. But then it blurts out of her mouth.

'What was with your bedroom, Dad? What was so secret about it? Why couldn't we go in there?'

He looks at her as if she has crossed some line but then takes a deep breath.

'Fair enough question, Girlie', he says, and gathers his thoughts for such a long time Carol wonders if he is OK but doesn't dare to break the silence.

'Your mother,' he says so quietly she has to lean towards him, 'felt that there was one space in the house where she could let down her guard and be with her fears and desperate neediness, where she could go back to her loveless childhood and feel the pain. And to be honest,' he says with obvious great difficulty, 'it was where I too could revisit that boyhood fear that my father was beating my mother to death and that I was next in line. It was our space of love and our space of horrors. We sometimes clung to each other all night like frightened children. We tried so hard to never let it out of that room and to never let any of you into it.'

Carol looks at him. She feels a surge of love so exquisite she can hardly bear it. She cherishes his honesty. She can see them curled up on that bed, young adults, clinging to each other, putting up the protection barriers so that all that happens in that room stayed in that room. But of course it didn't. She knows that now. It seeped out despite their best efforts.

Her dad clears his throat.

'So what got you through it?'

'Love. I think it was the love and knowing we could tell each other anything and still love each other. Each of us in our own way had periods of doubt and especially your mother. She was, at times, very fearful of losing herself, and me, and all of you. But somehow we managed to stay in love, despite it all. Is that what they call co-dependence now?'

'I don't care what they call it now.'

'But you should know, too, what happened after Robert got sick. I went to pieces. At first I denied it was happening. I could see he was depressed, but I kept thinking Gabby got like that sometimes, and look at her, she could pick herself up and go back to being her wonderful self. But when it didn't get better, and when the psychosis started, I felt so cheated of my beautiful boy. It was like I couldn't bear for him to be taken away from me.'

'So what did you do?'

'Not much. And that was the problem. I didn't help much at all. So Gabby just got stronger and stronger, and tried to comfort me while she took the main role in looking after Robert, and getting him the help he needed, and all the time kept the household going, and managed somehow to give Andrew the attention he needed when he got sick.'

'So she became the strong one?'

'Yes. But guess who was her greatest help. You, the most indulged and indulgent little thing, leaping into adolescence like you could do everything and anything you wanted, you watched your mother so intensely, you followed after her, sitting with Robert after she had to leave him to get the dinner, reading to him, or just listening to music with him, or just holding one of his big hands, and in your own little way, letting him know that someone else was there for him. Part of you was still such a kid, Girlie, and part of you suddenly grew up for him, and especially for her. I don't know if she could ever let you know how much that meant for her.'

And all at once, it starts. Big gasping sobs. He holds her tight. They don't say any more. They stay there on the big old swing seat until it stops and she walks home, amazed at the sudden realisation that she cannot remember anything about that time at all.

❋ ❋ ❋

Work for Carol becomes a welcome relief from being in her family. She has to fill in for ten days straight because the full time physio has taken leave. She does so with a feeling of gratitude that she has little time left for family matters. Or for Jack matters. It's all happening too fast. She loves the time she has with him. She likes his way of thinking, of having thought so many things through. She likes the way he takes her seriously and listens carefully to anything she wants to talk about. But, even putting aside his fears about flooding, she can't quite put her finger on it. Is it all happening too deep too fast? She has no idea. She hasn't done this for such a long time. In fact, she admits to herself, she hasn't done it at all like this before.

Almost two weeks go by before she goes around to her dad's place again with a casserole dish and a pudding for them to share. They have planned to pick his tomato crop which has grown totally out of hand in the late autumn heat, and despite his tying them up on taller and taller stakes, the plants are almost doubled over with the weight of more tomatoes than either of them have ever seen in anyone's back yard.

As they fill every fishing bucket he can lay his hand on, she is wondering what on earth they were going to do with all that produce. But not for long.

They sit on the swinging seat on the front verandah sipping their hard-earned beers. Two sprightly older women wave at him as they stride down the side passage of his house, carrying very large pots, with an air that they know exactly where they are going and why. Carol hears the back door bang as they enter the kitchen.

'Chrissie and Marge,' he says. 'From dancing.'

'Oh, don't they want to stop and say hello?'

'No, they want to get straight into it.'

'It?'

'Yes.' He looks sheepish. 'Tomato sauce for pasta.'

'Right, of course.'

They take their time, finishing their beers.

SIXTEEN

'Hi Andrew. How're things?'

'Hi Carol, good to hear from you. It's been a while, eh.'

'Yeah, thought it was time for a catchup. How's our boy?'

'Our boy is perfecting the art of being a total arsehole of a teenager, but I keep telling myself it's normal, and it's better he does it all now instead of as an immature adult like I was. I've taken a big stand to ban the bong.'

'Sounds like a new slogan – Ban the Bong.'

'Yeah, well it is around here. Hey, I've been meaning to thank you heaps for being with Dad. You know he just raves about you and how good it is to have you around, and how you have been such a help with Robert. He probably doesn't tell you but he certainly lets me know.'

Carol can hardly believe that she is actually being thanked.

'Well thanks for that. I feel quite privileged getting to know Dad, and he is unloading lots of history about him and Mum. It belongs to all of us, Andrew, not just me. But I don't know what to do with it. How to share it.'

She tries a new tack. 'Jennifer seems such a mess at the moment.'

'About Jennifer,' he says, 'sometimes I wish I weren't so far away. She really does need some help with John and all. Especially after the drama with the creek.'

'Yeah. Go on.'

'Well I guess you know that farmer who shares that pathetic little creek got really angry at John illegally pumping water at night and threatened to call the police.'

'Mmm.'

'You didn't know?'

'Not the details,' she lies, 'but I sort of put two and two together.'

'Apparently the old guy paid a visit to John one night, making threats, and then he pulled back when John suggested that the police might also be interested in the hydroponic crop his son was growing in the old shed. After lots of shouting they decided none of this was really police business after all.

'Shit.'

'It was all last straw for Jennifer. She had no idea that John was stealing creek water at night. She hates the way these grown up men can act like two bulls in the paddock and then suddenly switch and start acting act like some sort of gentlemen, like grazing aristocracy. She hates that John can get away with it. Andrew hardly stops to draw breath. Hey Carol ....'

'Yeah I'm still here.'

'There's something else, but I don't want you to say anything.'

'OK.'

'I think Jennifer is planning to leave John. To make a fresh start in the Blue Mountains. The school will give her a good deal if she wants to keep the twins there as day pupils and she is waiting for her share of the money to come in and then she can leave.'

'Oh my gosh. I never dreamt ...'

'She might talk to you about it soon but she sounds so embarrassed about it all. Like she is the one who has failed. Crazy.'

Carol sits stunned while Andrew goes on.

'Hey,' he says, 'before you go, Dad says he will be sending me my share of the sale of the house. Half a million will go a long way here. We're going to buy a holiday house on a lake across the border in Canada. It's only a few hours north of here. Come over. Fishing and swimming and kayaking in summer and even skating on it in the winter if the very cold weather comes back.'

'I'd really like that, Andrew. I really would.'

She feels she has to stop this call now and get her mind around Jennifer.

'Love to both your boys.'

Carol gives a big sigh as she thinks about the changes that Jennifer is making to her life . Jennifer, who so likes order in her life, who needs predictability, who would endure heaps to keep the marriage going.

And Andrew's other words keep circling in her brain. 'If the very cold weather comes back.' Has it really got like they don't expect the lake to freeze over as it does every winter? Is there no certainty about even lakes anymore?

❋ ❋ ❋

Andrew puts down the phone. He remembers that when Paul suggested he tell Carol she was doing so well being down there with their Dad, he had scoffed. These North Americans were so into praise. Lots of backslapping and gratitude. Lots of building up self esteem in kids. He hated it. 'Great shot, buddy' to the uncoordinated baseball player. 'You've got talent there,' to the tone deaf choir reject.

But, hey, it just worked. A crack had appeared, with Carol, 'like the crack in everything' as Leonard Cohen sings, 'That's how the light gets in.'

His ear had picked up Carol's slight gasp when he mentioned about not knowing about skating on the lake anymore. He knows only too well that it has been happening slowly over the past few years. Yes they got the occasional very cold winter, but mostly the ski fields were receding and the snow machines were brought in to do overtime so that the winter tourist season still happened. Everyone around there was taking it all for granted. The climate was changing.

Andrew finds it hard to keep his focus on the impacts and the seriousness of climate change as he luxuriates in the early morning sun warming up the glass on the big southern windows. He is blessedly alone, with Christopher at Lisa's, Paul out of town on business, and a morning free from teaching music at the nearby secondary school.

He lets his mind drift over the border to Canada. He had always wanted to move to Canada. Canada. He loved the sound. He loved the softness of their accents. And going there, it felt like visiting the old British Commonwealth cousins. He'd never got what was so 'united' about the USA.

But Lisa said she was a USA girl through and through so they'd compromised moving to the far north of Washington State, where he could always creep over the border when he had the urge not to be American. Now his boy is American, and Paul is American, half of his dual nationality is American, and he teaches American kids.

He wonders how long it takes to feel like you belong here. He's still a visitor. Just perching there. Especially at election time. He never has got a real understanding of the political system. He reckons that understanding primaries was linked to the DNA.

Perhaps, Andrew muses, it is time to take Christopher back to Australia for a summer holiday. Perhaps it is time to take Paul over and show him Mardi Gras. Perhaps it was getting together last summer that is giving him this urge to go home. To spend more time than just a week or ten days.

He wants to feel the strong sun on his body, hear the familiar twang, have lazy days finished off with fresh seafood and very cold beer. He wants to do some travelling with his boys into the Centre. It is there, he reminds himself, that you feel at one with being Australian. If you listen carefully you can hear the rocks resonate to an ancient key.

Andrew jumps up. He needed a jingle. His latest talent is composing for an advertising company and he received a request only that morning. He races into the bathroom, strips off and turns the shower taps on full.

Relax, he tells himself. He closes his eyes. He sways backwards and forwards on his toes letting the water cascade over his body. Patience. And, yeah, the lyrics are coming. Now for the music.

Andrew grabs a towel, and half dried he makes for his desk. Pulls out manuscript paper. Gets it down. Goes to the keyboard. Yes. A repeat here. A change of key there. Done.

He gets dressed and almost skips down the four blocks to the school.

SEVENTEEN

Carol paces up and down in her little cabin. Weeks have gone by since she has seen him. More days have gone by since that crazy phone call with his outburst about the coast flooding. Lots of phone calls since. A few exchanges about their every-day lives. A coolness has crept in, replacing the magic of those first weekends. Now he is coming.

Carol tidies up the cabin once again – two whole things out of place. She steps back from the small mirror on the bathroom door so that she can see most of herself. It's OK. It will do. She doesn't want to look too dressed up. She doesn't want to look too dressed down. She tries to turn around and still looking in the mirror to check if she is getting fat and wonders where the waistline has gone. She ties her hair back.

Then she hears his car in the driveway. She races out and they start hugging before he's even all out of the driver's seat. Hands touching bodies. Mouths devouring each other. In no time at all they are naked on the bed. She has never felt so hot. It's over too soon. Carol wishes it would go on for ever. They lie back panting, looking at each other.

'Well hello, you.'

'And hello, you. How've you been?'

'Pretty good. Missing you. How've you been?'

'Hungry.'

And they laugh and make love all over again. Slower.

They jump up and race across the road to the sea.

'It's cold,' she shouts to his back, trying to keep up.

'It should be colder now. The cold current hasn't come in yet this year. It's the same in Sydney. They can't remember when the water has stayed warm for so long.'

And they swim out. She's surprised how fit she's become over the past few weeks. Her swimming is stronger now. She feels like she could swim forever.

Over dinner he asks, 'So what's happening with that family of yours?'

'You really want to know that?'

'Yes, I do actually.'

'But how come we don't talk about yours?'

She could only just remember the Turner boys. They always seemed so much older than the O'Briens. She was curious now to find out what had happened to them all.

'OK then.' He said. 'First we'll order and then I'll give you the abridged version.

Mmm. I'll have the snapper. How about you? OK, two. Oh and this Chablis.'

He begins. 'Mum and Dad died a few years ago within a few months of each other. First Dad, stroke, then Mum, one big cardiac.'

'I'm sorry about that.'

'My brothers mostly live in Sydney and we get together quite often. I'm the only one without kids, so it's great when we all go on picnics or boating or whatever, as I can be the mad uncle who likes to play games with my nieces and nephews.'

He counts on his fingers, 'All eight of them. But now they don't have time for family outings, so I take them out to lunch one by one. It seem that they can tell uncle about things they don't want to discuss with their parents.'

'And your brothers? I used to get them all mixed up as a kid. You all seemed so alike.' She adds, 'to a little kid, anyway.'

'Can you remember any of them?' he asked, 'other than me?'

'Was there a Ken?'

'Very good. He's the eldest. He's a GP in Sydney, married and very straight. Any others?'

She tries but draws a complete blank about the other two brothers.

'Well, next is our artistic one, Mark, who makes documentary movies, and then there is me, very eligible academic, and last there is Terry, who earns heaps of money as a merchant banker and has bought a ski lodge to satisfy his lovely wife who teaches skiing. You do ski, don't you?'

'Er, no.' She wants to explain that snow is a bit scarce in the sub-tropics where she has spent all her adult life.

'Oh, you'll pick it up without any trouble, I'm sure.'

'I'm not so sure. My mum's skating genes certainly passed me by. I'm more of a solid ground sort of girl but I'd like to catch up with your brothers. They all sound very different.'

'Yeah, we were allowed to be different. Bit like your lot.'

'It's funny isn't it. We're both one of four kids, and we're both third one down.'

'Yes,' he says.

'Tell me about your place in Sydney?' The question just pops out. And as it does she realises there is so much she doesn't know about Jack.

'A few years back,' he says, 'I got sick and tired of living in rented apartments and it took ages for me to find the right one for me. I don't need much in the way of space, but I did have some rather different requirements. Can you guess what?'

She thinks of Jack's outburst about the coastal houses, but she doesn't really want to bring that up. So she just shrugs her shoulders and looks puzzled.

'My friendly estate agent said I was the only client he has ever had who had an altimeter app on his phone. I wanted at least 100m above sea level, but as hilly as Sydney is, especially in the eastern suburbs, above a hundred metres is very hard to find.'

'Really.'

'So I finally bought a place just down from the park behind the public school in Bellevue Hill. The park is very high and almost at my back yard, so most days I walk up to the top and sit there gazing down to the sea, a comfortable distance below.'

'Does it make you feel safe?'

'Just less unsafe.'

And they both think about that for a while.

'So what have you been up to?' he asks.

Such a simple question, but Carol feels stuck. She does not want to talk about her family. But she can't think of a dammed thing she has been doing, except perhaps work, that doesn't involve her family.

She thinks about all the signs that had been crowding in on her about climate change, and even that was still centred on her bloody family – her girl and the coal dust, Jonah and the timber, Andrew and the winter not being so cold any more, and Jennifer and John and their lives and their very psyches going apeshit trying to farm in the longest drought in living memory.

So she tries a pathetic 'not much', but feels like a teenager saying 'not much' when there is too much.

He waits, and then says, 'O good. I can keep talking about me. Would you like to hear about my new program at the gym?'

'Thanks.'

So she starts telling him about her doubts about staying down on the South Coast now that her dad seems to have finished telling her all he needed to tell and now that he had a few women taking over his kitchen.

'So I wonder what I am doing here, even if Brook wants to move down, I don't feel like waiting around for that to happen, if it does happen, and I am ready to look at what's next.'

'Well,' he says. 'I'm glad you did move down, or otherwise we would never have caught up with each other again.'

And then she smiles and reaches for his hand.

'So it's all been worth it, hasn't it? To meet a great catch like me?'

'I've been thinking,' she says, getting quite light headed, sipping her third glass of Chablis, 'about taking time off and driving up north. Catching up with friends. Join some coal seam gas demos.'

'That's your idea of a good time?' he asks, 'Coal seam gas demonstrations?'

'It's hard to explain', she says, trying to find the right words. 'It's part of the culture.'

'So why drive?' he asked with a sheepish grin. 'Train not good enough?'

'They stopped the train. But anyway, I need the sense of getting from here to there. I need to drive up the coast, and see the vegetation gradually change to sub-tropical. I need to do it slowly.'

She continues, 'When I was a child, and even sometimes now, I have flying dreams where I float above the landscape looking down at the houses and cars getting smaller and smaller the higher up I go. I can see where I am going like on a map, being so aware that the real expanse of space is up, while everyone down there thinks space spreads laterally around them. I can still get in touch with that feeling when

I am driving and I can float above my car and see the map of where I am.'

'In that case,' he says, 'I might just take a flight in a real plane and join you for a longish weekend. How would that be?'

'Sure. That would be so good. You can see another me.'

'This 'me' will do.'

Later that night, he surprises her by saying, 'I want to know what you really think about my climate change rave. About all these beach villages disappearing into the sea.'

Carol does not want this conversation. It intrudes into the romantic mood of the dinner. Her body is feeling lighter, younger, as she plays with the notion of moving out of her long relationship drought.

She stalls for time. He doesn't push her for an answer.

Eventually, she says, 'I guess I was taken aback by the suddenness and the intensity of it. Especially after finding the family beach house so locked in time. It's not that I don't doubt that all these things will happen. But I always think that it is not going to happen just yet.'

'Fair enough.'

She reaches for his hands across the table. 'But mostly, I got concerned about you. And I want to know more about how it affects you. Like all the time? Just sometimes? I want to know how present it is, in your life.'

He is listening. Attentively.

'I want to know if I should be concerned.'

'Fair enough,' he says. 'It comes and goes. But when it is there it is, ah, what's the word, it's visceral.'

'Yes, I can see that.'

'And, you know, you are right. I think most people can't contemplate it all happening on the coast in their life times. But I can. And it gets intense because sometimes I am the only one I know who can see it as a now thing. And the more people don't want to know that the more urgent it gets for me to talk about it.'

'Yes.'

'Only I stop talking about it, except to myself. I know that's not good. Now let's plan that trip north.'

'Yes.'

'Perhaps,' she says, 'I should call in on my way up north and visit your house on the hill. Perhaps I should get an idea of somewhere that is less unsafe.'

'Yes.'

* * *

Jack puts off the drive home. He hates the Sunday traffic back to Sydney. He lets himself into his parents' house, and settles down with a cold beer.

Restless, he heaves himself out of the chair and wanders around the house, trying to see it as it would have looked to Carol. He runs his hands over the heavy wooden dining table, glances at the line up of old photos on the mantle piece and visualises the lot as a prime display in the museum - 'suburban life last century.'

'Yes,' he agrees with himself, 'it could do with some new life.'

He settles back down with his beer.

He wonders about having invited himself to visit Carol when she takes her road trip to Byron Bay. It just came out. He didn't plan it at all.

Jack reminds himself that his life is the product of a few decades of serious planning. His planned transition from lawyer to academic. A good move. He enjoys his contact with students, especially the bright ones who challenge his own sureness about his entrenched ethical positions.

He looks back at his planned move into his apartment. So different to this house. A great bachelor pad that he has comfortably spread himself around in, with his large bed facing east so that he can see the first rays of sun, his well ordered study, his big screen he can watch football on with his mates on the weekends, his very male kitchen he can cook up a treat for his single and couple friends. He especially likes it when one of his nieces or nephews is in between houses and comes to take over the spare room for a while and then he loves it even more when they leave.

He wonders, as he so often does, if the time has come to give up his very solo existence. If he and Carol could make it work. If she would want to move back to Sydney after all this time. If she would manage to fit into his apartment and make it her home. He smiles as he pictures it, and realises how much he really would like to share his life with a woman, this woman.

'Traffic should be clearing by now,' he tells himself.

EIGHTEEN

Home. A giant magnet is pulling Carol's little car north. Home. Back up to the sub-tropics. Back up to her territory, her place. She is humming. She is relaxing into the long drive. Except for one thing. A promised visit to Jack's place in Sydney.

She tries but cannot quite put her finger on why the waves of anxiety wash over her. He wants her to see where he lives. So what could be so scary about that?

'So of course you will stop over on your way up north.'

'Of course.'

'It's not about just having a look you know.'

'Yes, I know.'

' I really want you to see it. I really want you to like it. Carol, I really want you to feel at home there.'

'Yes, I know.'

Doing the replay in her mind, Carol knows that he has a future in his mind.

'C'mon,' she tells herself. 'Let's get a bit of enthusiasm here.'

Several hours later, she parks outside the address he has given her. She looks up to the first floor. Modern. Schmick. Big windows. A long balcony suspended high in the canopy of the tall lillipilli trees. She gets out of her car with the sea breeze blowing in from the east. The huge Morton Bay figs in the park behind block out the western sun. It is cool. She shudders a little and wraps her light cardigan around her. The front door opens with a start before she has a chance to knock. And there he is. Smiling. Bending down to take her overnight bag.

'Come on up,' he says after a brief hug. He bounds up the stairs like an eager puppy. She follows. She walks in and gasps.

The living space is light and white and spacious, with a marble tiled floor and exquisite oriental rugs. Two large modern paintings stand out as the only bright colours on the only straight wall. In front of her the ceiling-high glass doors are folded back and she walks outside feeling the vertigo of being in the tree tops, looking out to the ocean across a sea of red-tiled roofs.

She gasps. 'Oh my gosh, it is so beautiful. It feels so high up. It feels like you can see forever.'

Jack smiles. 'Yes. Hey come and see the rest of it.'

She follows him obediently, back through the living room, where he waves towards the open kitchen area, saying 'kitchen', into the main bedroom also facing east to the sea. He proudly shows her the outdoor bath neatly concealed on the small balcony, the clean white en-suite, the immaculately ordered dressing room, and then across the living room again to the study and spare bedroom with its smaller white en-suite. All neat. All white. All minimalist. All marble tiled. All with luxurious rugs.

'So?'

'Jack, I had no idea.'

'But you like it.'

'It is beautiful. It really is very beautiful.'

Carol caught herself thinking, 'Thank goodness he didn't say - good girl.'

Later that night, they are lying in bed. He starts massaging her shoulders, hands wandering down to her breasts. Carol pictures the little cabin. She imagines they are back there. She starts to relax into his touch. She keeps her eyes closed. She is there and she is not there.

Over breakfast he says, 'Can you imagine living here? With me?'

And before she realises, out pops a 'No.'

It startles both of them.

'I mean, it's different. It doesn't feel like me. I'd kind of have to get used to it.'

'But it's me. You might have to kind of get used to me.'

'Yes.'

'I don't want to rush you.'

'No.'

'I've booked my flights to Byron Bay. I've never been there. I must be just about the only person I know who hasn't.'

He needs to get ready for work. She needs to get back into her car.

She gives a big sigh as she finally gets out of the traffic. It's over an hour till she finally gets onto the northern freeway. She's not just travelling to, she is very much travelling from. From her Dad and his stories of horrible childhoods. From her sadness about Robert and what he could have, should have become. From Jennifer and the drought. Now there's a new one to run from. Marble floors and stark white walls and the unbearable neatness of it all, and Jack himself who is such a puzzle with the museum of his parents' house at one extreme and this at the other. And she wants to run from his certainty that they could live together when they hardly know each other and his incredible insight about some things and incredible lack of insight about others. Perhaps he wants to rush into this new life before the flood takes his coastal retreat. Perhaps it's his timing that's all screwed up. Perhaps he's suddenly realised he's on the wrong side of middle age and he'd better get his escape route to ageing planned and underway.

Not kind, she says to herself. Not kind.

She turns the music on in her phone and it kicks in with Janis Joplin. She tries to harmonise with the vocals, loudly, sometimes getting it but what the hell, there's just her. Hey that feels good. Just her.

The hours slip by. The old question pops up. Does she divert from the freeway to a little town and try for a decent cup of coffee and non-junk food or does she give in to the golden arches? She does both. Decent coffee in the little town. Indecent junk at McDonalds.

Midday and she turns on ABC radio. And then she wishes she hadn't.

News from the aptly named Cape Grim in Tasmania where the monitoring site has recorded the first baseline reading of 400 parts per million per hour of atmospheric carbon dioxide in the southern hemisphere. That's tipping point. That's the point we never wanted to get to. That's the point of no return.

She listens to the discussion.

Four hundred has been reached in the northern hemisphere at times, but there is more land mass there and more vegetation and so there is more variation with highs in winter dropping back down in spring.

Now she waits for the inevitable balanced view that the ABC has to pretend to have so that it keeps its government funding.

It's just a number, 400. So it's one more than 399 and one less than 401. So what?

'So what?' Carol argues with them. It might be just a number, but so was the size of the big hole in the ozone layer before they banned CFCs. So is the record highest temperature of the ocean. So is the rate of melting of the Arctic ice.

'Don't tell me it's just a number,' she shouts at the car radio.

'History,' Mr Reasonable says, 'will be the only real test.'

'Yeah,' she screams. 'Well history might just be a bit too late, you bastard.'

The interviewer now turns to the Minister and the Shadow Minister for the Environment and asks them if they still support the big new proposed coal mines in NSW and Queensland.

'Oh yes. Well, it is a state decision, after all,' says one.

'No,' lies the other.

She can't tell which is which.

'Will most of this coal be for export?' asks the interviewer.

'Even if we export the stuff, it's still a fossil fuel, you fuckwit!' They take no notice.

She hears a familiar beeping coming from her navigator. Way over the speed limit. She cuts back. Please no speed cameras. She promises to be good.

How about some more music.

Carol hits randomly and starts singing along with Brad from the Rocky Horror Show,

'So baby don't cry like there's no tomorrow
After the night there's a brand new day ay ay ay ay.'

'Spot on Brad,' she says out loud. 'They all behave like there's no tomorrow.'

'And that's half the trouble,' she goes on to tell herself. 'There's no such thing as a brand new day ay ay ay ay.'

The day goes by. The night is spent in a motel off the highway. She gets there early so that she can open the door and the window and let out the smell of cleaning agents and disinfectants that is the specialty of cheap motels. She removes the 50% polyester sheets and replaces them with her own 100% cotton ones. She rips off the paper ribbon that tells her that her toilet has been cleaned for her protection. She walks into town for a surprisingly good Indian curry.

As she returns to the motel, Carol notices the confused frangipani growing in the front yard and sees that while it is losing half of its big leaves, as it should at this time of year, it is also covered in a mass of new buds, which it definitely should not be doing at this time of year. She doesn't know whether to offer it her condolences and apologies on behalf of the humans, or tell it to get real and decide whether it's being deciduous in autumn or flowering in spring but it can't do both.

Carol checks her phone for messages and returns none of them. Her emails remain in their undisturbed virgin state. She crashes into bed and waits for the visual echo of the highway to disappear from behind her closed eyes.

Just as she is dropping off, Jack phones.

'Hi you.'

'Hi you.'

'How was the drive?'

'Oh, good so far. Just cruised along.'

'You sound sleepy. Did I wake you?'

'No.'

'Well you get a good night's sleep.'

'Yes. Ta. G'night.'

Carol falls immediately into a deep sleep.

Towards noon next day, she feels the thrill of driving back into her home town. She can hardly believe it is only a few months since she left. She is startled anew by the sharp vivid colours of the vegetation. Subtropics. Ahhh.

She gratefully gets out of the car and stretches her arms up to the sky, swaying from side to side at the waist until she feels a gentle thump on her back.

'Hi.' She turns around with delight at the sight of her old friend. 'Cindy!' she shouts. They hug. 'Time for a coffee?'

'Sure,' she says, 'let's make it lunch.'

Lunch lasts for hours. Cindy listens with interest to Carol's abridged version of her family, and then shows much more enthusiasm when Carol starts telling her about Jack.

Carol listens to Cindy's catch up from the last few months and what's been happening with their friends. Carol hears all about the organised community action against coal seam gas, and how they have driven, at least for now, one of the big exploration companies out of the area. She glows with pride. This is my tribe. I am home.

But she also hears the down side. What's been happening in the town. How the state government is allowing more and more big developments. How the town is in traffic gridlock, how the rents are sky-rocketing now so that so many people are earning a bit extra on the side with Airbnb. How investors are favouring tourist rentals instead of renting to locals. How renters like her can't afford to live in this town any more, or even nearby towns and villages and how people like her are having to look elsewhere even though they get some part-time work here, love it here, and have their kids going to school and TAFE around here.

'On top of that,' Cindy tells her, 'the local water supply dam is nearly empty and they had to make up a higher level of water restrictions. So we all have buckets in our showers, buckets for our washing machine pump-outs.'

Carol and Cindy take off their shoes and walk along the beach, along the hard wet sand, hardly even noticing the waves splashing their clothes till they are dripping wet below the knees. Carol feels a deep sense of belonging on this beach. As they turn back she can see the line up of the Border Ranges, little more than hills really, against the western sky. Her body luxuriates in the unseasonal warmth of the late autumn afternoon, as the shallows turn pink and yellow. Home.

She has been listening carefully to what Cindy has been saying about the changes. She reminds herself that it is always changing and has been changing since she first arrived three decades ago. OK, now it's changing faster. The old crowd moves out and the glitterati move in. But the beautiful beach is the same. Carol closes her eyes and can visualise high-rise buildings dotted around the foreshores turning the bay into a Gold Coast look alike. Yeah, she sighs, of course they can stuff this special place. Fucking growth and greed and a state government with a merchant banker mentality.

Then she remembers to ask Cindy how her business is going. Cindy, single mum, struggling on the pension with some café shift work, has started up her own internet business, called 'Minders', where she links up local people who are forever going away for extended holidays and don't want to rent or Airbnb their places. They don't care about the money but want someone reliable to move in to look after the place and do whatever is necessary, like some gardening, or walking the dog, or feeding the cat. Cindy charges a minder fee and the minder pays a nominal amount. Cindy, as much as anyone, is surprised by her own success. Some of her otherwise homeless friends have bookings that cover them for the whole year.

Carol feels happy for her that she has managed to get her life together in this challenging community, where jobs are scarce and foreign backpackers too available for low paid work.

Cindy tells her that she has found a two week mind for her. All she has to do is take the new grandbaby for a long walk in her pram most days. Oh, and feed the cats.

'And not only that,' she says. 'We have a special homecoming surprise for you,' she says. 'Our women's group is meeting at my place tonight. Not too tired, I hope. Oh, and your choice of topic.'

'Don't seem to have any other plans,' Carol tells her.

They hug goodbye for a long time.

She's almost forgotten the Far North Coast long hugs.

Before heading off for Cindy's place, Carol turns towards the lighthouse hill, and starts walking up the bush track through the regrowth coastal forest. She smiles at the brush turkey crossing the path, neck stretched out, in a big hurry, diving behind the tree ferns and Bangalow palms. She puts her mind to the gathering that night and what she wants to open up with her women friends. It has been months. She has no idea what themes they have been discussing. Nothing comes to her as she starts puffing up the steep incline.

In a few hundred metres, Carol knows the climb will have been all worthwhile. She reaches the top, in full view of the deep autumn blue of the Pacific Ocean. The ocean is swirling and crashing on the rocks far below on one side of the lighthouse and on the other the long curve of the white sand borders the sparkling water of the bay. Straight ahead is the endless horizon of the Pacific Ocean. She notices a splash and fixes her eyes on that patch of water, waiting. Yes. Excitement runs through her body. Whales on their yearly migration to give birth in the warm waters of Harvey Bay. This place is still truly paradise.

That night all five women arrive on time. They kiss and do their long long hugs. They sneak in just a little small talk before starting the group. They sit cross-legged on cushions on the floor, facing the low table with the lit candle, surrounded by fresh flowers. Cindy leads the chanting and they close their eyes and join their voices into wondrously harmonious 'Oms.' They stay there in silence for a while, feeling totally present in this space, with their long history of sharing their stories, hopes, pain and joys.

They open their eyes and they look towards Carol with expectation.

'Siblings. Tonight I am offering Siblings.

A long pause. 'Let's go round and say how you have been affected by your siblings and how that is for you, now.'

So they do. Except of course for Trish who has no siblings and who talks about how that affected her sense of self. But then they dig deeper, as they ritualistically do, as Carol fields the gentle but probing questions, as best she can.

They ask about hers. About her being in third place. About lines of alliance between Jennifer and Andrew and between her and Robert. And about getting together as adults after so long, and with their mother having just died.

Carol's dilemmas bring up Cindy's big sister memories of mothering her little twin sisters when her mother had to go back to work.

But mostly they talk about differences. How they feel different from their siblings. I'm not musical like her. I'm the only one who likes distance running. As the only girl I had to be tough to join in their games. She was always my mum's favourite, but I didn't really mind because I was my dad's.

Several hours later, they share their cakes and chai teas and make light and silly talk. And then the big hugs of goodbye.

Carol creeps away to Cindy's spare bed. She has a whole lot to think about. Like why was she so curious about sibling stuff that she had to make it tonight's topic? Their questions stick about her mother's death. How they could be physically together, but how come they didn't comfort each other? And then it hits her. They all lick their wounds in private. How weird it that? They all just shove it down and stow it away. Jennifer. Robert. Andrew. Herself. Even their dad. Unreachable.

In Cindy's spare bed, Carol drops into a half sleep, questions finally banished and replaced with a glowing gratitude for the trust and honesty of her close women friends.

NINETEEN

In the last few days of her visit, Jack arrives from Sydney. They have given themselves the luxury of two nights in a tourist apartment across the park from the main beach. They are lying in the king-sized bed looking north through the big glass sliding doors. The sea is bright blue on this lazy Saturday morning.

Newspapers read, coffee and croissants done, they drive inland. Carol wants to show him her favourite bit of rainforest a few hours north west of Byron Bay. In the car she rabbits on about how, before her time here, there was an established counter culture of hippies and conservationists who pioneered rainforest demonstrations. Jack asks questions she finds impossible to answer. He wants to know what happened to the hippies who were arrested. He wants to know if their actions had an effect on the legislation about conservation. He's interested in all the legal details she never paid any attention to. They park the car and walk across the road to the beginning of the track. A few steps in and it is another world. They have passed through an invisible curtain and once inside the air is moist, the smell is dank but sweet, and their eyes slowly move up and up to the tops of the giant trees, with their complex decorations of vines, epiphyte ferns, mosses and lichens. The dense canopy filters the sunlight into ever changing patterns on the leaf litter at their feet. The track is easy to follow because the bush on either side is almost impossible to walk through.

They walk in silent awe.

As they climb they can hear the rushing of the creek, and pass small pools surrounded by ferns and palms. Flowers and berries of extraordinarily bright colours appear randomly. The top pool is thankfully empty of people, and they strip and plunge into the freezing water for just a few minutes of frantic splashing, and then lie on the rocks to dry off.

On the drive back, Jack looks around at the hills thick with rainforest, 'Looks like there's plenty of that forest left around here.'

'Mmm,' she replies. 'Most of that is regrowth. Regrowth happens quickly up here. Last century, or it might be the one before by now, all of that was cleared when the big trees were felled for timber and shipped to Sydney so that they could decorate the sandstone public buildings in the cities and the mansions of the wealthy. Then of course the settlers up here flattened the rest for cows and bananas.'

She's on a roll. 'The Big Scrub' she goes on, 'was huge. It went all the way from these hills to the coast. After the big clearing, the run-off from the bare hills silted up the wide inland rivers so that the steam boats couldn't make it to the inland towns anymore. Clearing ancient rainforest, wiping out species, stuffing up the rivers, they managed to do the lot.'

'Let's stop and get some food,' he says.

Carol realises that she has been preaching. 'Sure.'

They pull over at the next town, and find a hippy looking café, smiling at the rough chairs, all different, the stars painted on the ceiling, and the parachute silk on the far wall.

She wants to tell him about the first forest protesters. The people who dragged giant concrete pipes to block the logging roads. The people who stayed on platforms high up in the biggest loggable trees. The people who were arrested time and time again. The people who were her heroes and who inspired her to join the movement and to do outrageous acts.

As they leave the hills and drive back east to the coastal strip, she puts him on notice.

'I want to hear sometime about your passions.'

He looks at her with no hint of a smile. 'Refugees,' he says. 'Asylum seekers. Detention centres. Manus Island and Nauru. Oh,' he adds, 'and then there are the disadvantaged kids in third world countries where life is too hard and not enough fun.'

Carol waits.

'There's more to me than flooding, you know. Inside there beats a big social justice heart.'

She smiles at the way he can put himself down and up at the same time. She doesn't know anyone else quite like that.

Back at the coast, they lie on the bed and look at the sky above the beach greying over with big clouds.

Her phone tells her there is a news bulletin. She doesn't want news bulletins on her phone but she doesn't know how to turn them off. She especially does not want bulletins this magnificent Saturday, but as she glances at her phone's face, it is telling her that there is a low pressure off the coast with wind speeds in excess of 200 km/h. It is moving westward towards the southern Queensland coast at about 7 km per hour.

Carol quickly tunes into the local radio station that is repeating the warning and telling them to keep listening for updates for northern NSW. It's telling them that the low pressure is still out to sea, but that they can expect high winds, and with the high tide, there are warnings to stay off the beaches.

'That's us,' she says, and then feels ridiculous. Jack reminds her gently that he does happen to know where he is.

It's mid afternoon and they have a few hours before the cyclone arrives somewhere close by. She still calls them cyclones. Two hundred km per hour winds still sound like a cyclone.

'Have you been in one before?' he asks.

'Not right in the middle of one. We mostly get the sides or the ends of them. But I've been in winds of 150 with heavy rain, and the rain comes sideways as well as down, and it does lots of damage to trees and roofs and power-lines and cars.'

Cars. She suddenly remembers her car is under the car port of this block of units, and wonders if she should move it to the underground car park.

'But if the electricity is cut,' she thinks out loud, 'I wonder if the pumps could keep the water level down in the underground car park. I have no idea if there is a generator.'

'Why would they need a generator?'

'The basement here fills up with water unless the pumps are going.'

Jack looks decidedly uncomfortable. He gets up and starts pacing around the room. His eyes on the floor. He does not answer her query 'Are you OK?' Her mind starts darting around searching for memories, information, whatever about panic attacks. But she keeps drawing blanks. She's never had one. She's never seen one. She's only heard of them and then not paid nearly enough attention. But she knows she has to take charge. OK then. She can at least do that.

'I've heard the bathroom is a safe place,' she says. 'How about we have a shower.'

He stops pacing. She goes up to him and slowly starts removing his shorts. He bends down so that she can peel his T-shirt off. She turns on the shower hard in the en-suite, and quickly steps out of her own shorts, flinging her T-shirt and undies in the corner. Slowly she leads him into the bathroom. He is compliant, like a big subdued child. By now he is very pale. He staggers, holding his hand over his mouth as if to stop the dry retching. Carol, totally unsure about what she is doing, keeps touching him, rubbing her hands smoothly over his soapy body. He sinks to the corner of the shower. Covers his face with his hands. And just shudders. Big shudders.

'This is not working,' she says out loud, helps him to his feet, grabs a few towels and leads him to the bed, laying the towels down. He curls up facing the wall. She curls up behind him, stroking his head, making soothing noises, trying to ignore the stirring in her clit as she feels his wet body leaning into hers, trying to ignore the shrill sound of the wind, lashing the big glass doors. She does not dare to turn on the radio for the latest bulletin. He rolls over and buries his head in her breasts. They lie still. Timeless. At last she hears his breathing slowly returning to nearly normal. She feels an immense surge of love for Jack, for his vulnerability, for his closeness. He starts to stir. He lifts his head away from her breasts and focuses on her face with a trace of a smile. They start stroking each other. She feels his hands on her breasts, moving down over her stomach. It happens oh so slowly. It happens oh so quietly. The bed feels like a life raft in the sea of the surging storm.

They lie back on the damp towels and look out towards the sea. It's almost dark a few hours before it is meant to be dark. The sky is full of low dark clouds and the wind is getting fiercer.

She tunes back into the local radio station. The warning bulletins are almost constant now.

Suddenly the rain starts. It pelts down with such force that they have to turn up the the radio. The wind is getting stronger and stronger. In the little light left they can see the trees outside bending ominously and the bay turning into turbulent white water. The glass in the large sliding doors is beginning to pulse in and out with the strong gusts of wind. They slide under the bed covers and hold each other tight. She can feel his body trembling.

He lies on his back, eyes fixed on the ceiling. She slides out quietly, as if it matters that any noise she makes could be heard above the howling and screeching of the wind, the noise of the rain battering the roof and the perilously close pounding of the sea. She closes the curtains, takes out all their leftover food and with a little help from the leftover wine she starts to put a meal together. The radio, now in hushed tones, tells her that the winds have been downgraded from five to four, and the low pressure system, with its centre still just off shore, is hovering.

It will be a long night.

When Jack stirs, she suggests their candle-lit dinner. He's just managing to hold it together. They eat in silence, knowing that they could only hear each other by shouting. Carol knows she can't shout without sounding angry and angry she most definitely is not. Jack is still pale and damp, but picks at the meal and does better on the wine.

Two very stupid movies later, they are fast asleep.

They wake early and pull aside the curtains. She looks at him. He is definitely a better colour. He smiles. 'Hello you.' 'Hello you.' She doesn't want to talk about his fear. Not today. And probably not for quite a while.

The wind has dropped but the rain is still pelting down. The waves are thrashing loudly against the sand dunes. Out on the balcony they can see that the park in front is a mess of fallen branches and stripped leaves. The road is littered with rubbish from bins that have been tossed about. Water covers all but the middle of the road and spreads over the gutter to the footpaths either side.

Carol needs to get outside. She suggests a walk in the rain. He suggests they turn on the radio for warnings. They get an endless list of which creeks and rivers are flooded at which points, which roads are cut, which communities have been evacuated during the night, and where winds are doing more damage further south.

They put on their rain gear and venture out. She wants urgently to go to her house, in the older and flat part of the town. She tells him that it isn't strictly in the flood plain, but flood plain maps haven't been too reliable during the big wets of recent years. She says it's an easy walk.

They pick their way on the high ground avoiding the swirling gutters and big puddles, but in no time at all their shoes are soaked through and useless. People are out. They grin and say hi to each other, like they recognise fellow survivors of the night. Kids are riding the flooded gutters on boogie boards. The town looks drenched, but the sand dunes have held, and unlike some previous storms, the business centre of town has escaped serious flooding.

She stands outside her small wooden cottage that sits well back in the block, behind a mini-forest of densely planted trees. The garden looks violated. Small trees lie flat on the ground. Larger trees, that have pushed their tap roots deep into the fertile layer below the sand, have been stripped of most of their leaves. They will recover, she tells Jack, and herself. The palms are fine. As are the casuarinas. The banana and papaya trees in the side passage are sadly lying prone in the large puddles. She feels the familiar love she holds dearly for this little house. It's what she rented when she moved into town as a newly single mother with Jonah and Brook. It's what she bought with her small deposit, at a time when little old wooden houses in this town were still affordable. It's where she found her new friends, her close neighbours who had lived there for decades, and her community with every possibly imaginable type of yoga, healing and alternative medicine and with every possibly imaginable type of activity from meditation to dune care. It was where her children could run free, explore the bush and swim in the ocean, and know there were at least half a dozen houses they could go to in the street if their mother was late home from work.

Ted and Jo, her tenants, are already in the back-yard, surveying the mess as she puts her head around the corner of the house. They walk around the yard. Carol stands on the outdoor table trying to get a view of the roof to make sure it is all still there. Jack offers to get up there instead, and proclaims all roof accounted for. They all clap.

They suggest a coffee. They sit around, and eat home-made oat cakes and drink coffee and talk about what a miracle it is that this old house has no leaks, and although the water was lapping at houses a few doors down, this house on its slight rise has been spared. Carol strikes a deal with them doing the clean up and replanting in lieu of a few weeks' rent, and then Jack remembers they have to see if the planes are able to land at the nearby airport for his afternoon booking.

She takes a last look at her place. As they walk back she looks around at this old part of town where more and more old wooden cottages are being sacrificed for look alike blocks of holiday units and she wonders how long it will be before her street loses its familiar charm.

The rain is easing. 'This is just like rain that comes in the afternoon in the wet season,' she says.

'Wet season?'

'Yeah, sub-tropics.'

'Of course.'

But Carol can see this is a whole other world for Jack. Wet seasons. Tenants that ask you in for breakfast. Cyclonic winds that are called low pressure systems. Talk of generators in case the power goes off. Twenty-four hour pumps in underground car parks. Fixing up the yard instead of rent.

And as she gets an inkling of what is going on in his head, her head is jumping with questions. Do I want to come back here to live? Do I want to live somewhere where the weather extremes of today keep breaking yesterday's records? Where it matters that the El Ninos are getting so much drier that our local water supply runs out. And it matters that the La Ninas are getting wetter and the high tides are getting higher because the dunes are certainly not. And where it matters that the bush fires are getting hotter and more severe in the very bushland that surrounds us.

They check the flights again. They pack up. She drives Jack to the airport. He is in much better spirits now that he is on his way out of there.

They talk all the way.

He starts with, 'How come you didn't seem so fearful of the high winds last night?'

Carol stops to think about that and stops herself from saying, 'Well I guess you made up for me.'

Instead she says, 'Well I did find it scary but I didn't feel in danger. I knew we could always stay in the bathroom, where we would be safer if it got really rough, and I guess I trusted the wind wasn't strong enough to lift the roof tiles, and there were no big trees nearby to come crashing down.'

Jack was quiet, so she adds, 'Anyone living up here for a long times experiences a few of these, and the first is the worst and then you realise everyone comes through.'

'Well, little miss optimism, look at what's been happening lately overseas. Everyone doesn't come through anymore because with the warming of the oceans these cyclones are getting bigger and more frequent and the damage is worse that we could possibly have imagined.'

Carol nods, wary at the sudden change in mood. True.

'Where have you been?'

She shrugs.

'Don't you watch the news anymore?'

'Not if I can help it,' she says. 'I don't like the news anymore.'

'So,' she adds reluctantly, 'tell me what was going on for you last night.'

It is his turn to be silent. But eventually he begins.

'It's not just last night. But you know that. It's with me a lot of the time. I call it my big red dog. It's on a leash, on a choker chain. I pull on him hard and he walks by my side, always pulling against the chain, always trying to get ahead of me but I hold him tight because, when he does get ahead he gets stronger and then I can't hold him back anymore, and he runs and I have to run after him, however fast he runs, wherever he goes, through crowds, forests, wherever.'

'How scary. And is that what happened last night?'

'Yes.'

'Does he have a name?'

'Zeus.'

Carol struggles to remember the tattered family copy of 'Greek and Roman Myths'.

'Mmm.'

'And I guess you expected that I would be the tough guy and protect you from whatever might happen ...'

And she laughs. 'I don't need a tough guy.'

She finds some middle ground. 'It's only on the outside that I seem tough.'

And as she says it, she thinks it is probably true. That as a single mum she had learnt to have a tough outside. She could chop wood, kill spiders and play soccer.

'So what do you fear, Carol?' he asks.

'That's a hard one.' She thinks hard.

'Do you want to know what I think you are afraid of?' he asks.

Carol does not like where this is going.

'OK, yes. What do you think?'

'You,' he says, 'my little love, are afraid of commitment.'

'Commitment?' She stops. Looks across at him. 'Commitment? I suppose that's zero commitment that I'm living down with my dad, hanging in there hearing all the stories of my parents' terrible childhoods, making sure he's looking after himself.'

'Yes.' He softens. 'It's great that you are doing that. Helping him get over the loss of your mother. Yes. That's commitment. But how about commitment to a relationship?'

'You mean to you, don't you.'

'Yes. To me and to a relationship.'

'Well how do you figure I'm missing commitment of that?'

'It seems I'm the only one who talks about us having a future together. Your future is wanting to get your brother and sister to share Robert and all his problems. Your future is Brook getting out of the coal country into a safe place and having children. Your future …'

'Stop. I get it.' She goes on, 'Look we've just got different timings. What you want you want now. I take a bit more time. That's all.'

'No. I don't think that's all.'

'Well that's pretty obvious.'

After a while he says,

'Look Carol. I'm sorry if I've upset you. We all carry stuff. I don't know where my big fears come from and I do know I go to pieces when they get control of me. I also know I have finally found someone I really want to share the rest of my life with. It's OK if it takes a bit longer for you. But are you just a bit of the way there?'

She starts to cry. She hates crying while she is driving and makes an effort to stop.

'Nobody has wanted me like that for so long. I don't think I know what to do with it.'

She knows he's right. It's her family thing. Now that her dad seems OK, it is Robert, and when it isn't Robert it will be Brook. And she is just now facing the legacy of her parents' childhood, their shared secret suffering and her mother's depression. She is only just starting to accept that they all carry something from that. Like is that why Jennifer seems so cold? Why Andrew so detached? Robert mad? No. She stops herself. Robert just went mad. And me, she wonders. Am I damaged and don't even know it?

'Sometimes,' she manages, longing for her thumb, 'it's hard.'

'We all have hard, sometimes,' he says. 'How about when it's hard you let me in? Is there any room there to let me in?'

'Yes. There's room.'

'I think,' she says as she gets a flash of messing up his clean white neat tidy home in the sky, 'we both have to make a bit of room.' And adds, 'Hey, that's talking future, isn't it?'

'Yes. That's talking future.'

Suddenly they are there at the airport.

He must have caught the North Coast big hugs, because he holds her so tight for much longer than usual and says, 'Let's reverse the weekends for a while. How about you come to

Sydney instead. There's a lot more to do there in winter. And we can let slip a few more little mentions about a future.'

'Sure, why not?'

Carol starts the long drive home trying to imagine herself there. Perhaps she could start on the spare room. Not a bright pink. Just a nice warm greyish pink. Just one wall to start with.

She turns on the radio. A second series of low pressures has hit Queensland and the inland rivers are in flood. Great. The NSW coastal rivers are in flood too. She realises that if she leaves now she can head west to the inland highway and come down southwards through the mountain ranges before the flood cuts the roads.

Carol stops and checks the weather map on her phone. The coastal rain pattern extends from the Queensland border into Victoria. It extends to the south west of the state, right over the length of the Murrumbidgee River. She dials Jennifer.

'It's broken, Carol,' she screams down the phone. 'The drought's broken. The creeks are all up and we keep running outside and getting ourselves drenched.'

With some difficulty, Carol pictures them, her big sister and John, dancing in the heavy downpour.

'That's great, Jen. I am so happy for you.'

'John's dad says we're in for a big flood.'

'Really?'

'Yeah, but I don't care. I'd better go.'

'Bye'.

Carol pictures the inland rivers swelling with the new rain, and breaking their banks to run across the flat western plains. She remembers a camping trip out west when a drought broke, seeing the mighty Darling, suddenly change from being a dry river bed back to a raging torrent. First they heard and then saw the wave of water coming down gathering width and height as they watched it carrying dead branches and brown mud. They said it had taken three days to come down from the Queensland border.

Now she imagines the mass of dry cracked farm land, the failed crop-lands and the bare pastures across the eastern states gradually filling up with fresh water from the inland rivers as they run anew and the huge artificial reservoirs on the big cotton farms filling and running over, and the rain still pelting down, filling creeks, flooding roads, and isolating small farming communities for months.

She thinks if John's dad is right, and he probably is, then John and Jennifer are just going from one environmental disaster to another. Yes, the droughts and floods are getting longer and more intense, but you'd think they could leave a bit of breathing space in between.

But for now, she just wants to get through before the rivers flood. She desperately wants to see her girl.

TWENTY

Carol loves this mountain route through the Great Dividing Range that separates the coastal plains on the east from the western slopes. She loves the inland towns it passes though. Old, by Australia's short time scale. So 'country'. Bakeries with lamingtons and pink topped current buns. Wide awnings to shade the footpaths. Utes with kelpies in the back, waiting patiently for the farmers to return from doing business or from the pub.

She stops for petrol and to phone her girl, to let her know she will be there in time for dinner, and that she wants to stay the night. Brook is ecstatic. She says Todd is away on a training course so there will be just the two of them.

Towards sunset Carol turns off the main highway, windscreen wipers doing double time. She can just see the landscape of farmland sprinkled with the unnatural metal towers that spell coal seam gas. And then, suddenly the rain eases and there appears before her the vast spectacle of a huge open-cut coal mine. A mass of black hills surrounding hectares of a wide black hole, expansive dams filled with bluish greenish water and she can just make out a train with its one kilometre long trail of open wagons that so freak Brook out.

At last she turns up the long rough driveway to the farmhouse, the manager's cottage that comes with Brook's job. Carol knows that Brook will hear her approach as she bumps up the hill. She is waiting, freshly showered, blond hair pulled back, looking tall and healthy, with her father's perfect oval face, her darling girl.

They talk. They talk while Brook shows her the improvements they have made to the house. They talk while Brook puts the finishing touches to dinner. They talk while they eat, and then they sit down to talk some more.

Carol notices that Brook seems much calmer than when they spoke on the phone about the coal. Brook says, yes, she had a big melt down, and Todd, being Todd just let her ride through it, till she came out the other end and then they looked more calmly at planning their move away from the coal instead of bolting, which, anyway, Todd had no intention of doing.

'He's over managing land rehabilitation for the mines. He says it's a pretend sort of job as a lot more than just the surface land has been affected.'

'And how are you about that?'

'Oh, I just want to be close enough to a uni to get proper qualifications. I'm over doing courses online. I might as well be a student if I am going to be pregnant and have little ones.'

She added, 'I want an agriculture degree, Mum. I want to do it face to face and first hand. We're looking at Western Sydney Uni and moving down to the foot of the Blue Mountains. Todd's already applying for jobs down there. And anyway,' she adds, 'it's less risky, you know, from sea rise. We've done a total rethink about the coast. I suppose, you know about Aunt Jen. She is moving to the Blue Mountains.'

'How did you know that?' Carol looks across and sees her daughter sitting straight, a sure sign she is struggling with what to say next.

'Mum, I do talk to Aunt Jen. We talk a lot about the intensity of climate change right now in our rural communities. How this big drought is affecting every single person, on the land and in the town as well. I think Todd is getting through to John, too. They both come from farming families. They don't say much but at least they do talk.

'I just spoke to Jen,' Carol says, feeling she is somehow competing with Brook and not wanting to compete with her at all. 'The drought's broken'.

'So's her marriage. Totally broken. Despite John's efforts to patch things up, she's leaving, Mum, just as soon as the money comes through from Grandad. She's actually frightened of having the twins living with her after all this time. She wants me and Todd to visit often on weekends. And we'll be quite close.'

Carol cannot suppress these stirrings. Why does she feel uncomfortably jealous? She doesn't want to be close to Jennifer or her kids. So why doesn't she want Brook to be close? She doesn't want Brook closer to Jennifer when she has a baby. She wants to be the one who is closest.

Just as she is telling herself not to be so stupid, Brook moves over and puts her arms around Carol.

'Mum,' she says, 'Aunt Jen will never ever replace you. We need to go where Todd can get work, where we can afford to live, and where I can have a career and a few kids. Look at us together now. We can stay close no matter where we are.'

'Well,' Carol finally says, 'I might be moving to Sydney so we won't be all that far apart after all.'

'You think you have a secret, don't you Mum. But we all know about Jack. Grandad thinks it's just what you need.'

'Oh, does he now,' and she quickly changes the subject. 'So Jonah's moving too.'

They talk about Jonah, and Brook says how it was hard for her growing up because Jonah was so good, she was the one to cause all the trouble at home, and how that all changed after the lost baby thing.

'Can we talk about the lost baby thing?' she asks.

'Of course. What do you want to know?'

'It was weird. It sort of changed our lives around but I never did understand why. I get that finding a new born baby was pretty dramatic, but …'

'I was really shaken by that baby. The shock of seeing it so helpless and, well, dumped. Abandoned. It opened me up. It made me cry deep sobs that surprised even me. It touched my sense of abandonment, like I had been abandoned too.'

'But you weren't ever abandoned were you?'

Yes. No. Yes. No. Carol knows she was never abandoned. But ….

'We need to go back a few steps. Grandad's been telling me about how both he and your grandmother had such difficult childhoods, but especially how she was never really loved and although they could love each other, somehow, for her it never really made up for the damage.'

'Go on.'

'So I can remember there were times when she needed to be all by herself, and looking back I can see she went into deep depression.'

'So does that mean that you felt abandoned?'

'Well there were times when she wasn't there for us.'

'So where does the abandoned baby fit?'

'I felt such pain for that baby. I didn't want to hand her over to the police. I wanted to take her home and look after her, but I knew that was just crazy stuff. It put me into such a vulnerable space. Open. Raw. Not sure about anything anymore. Certainly not sure about how well I was mothering, especially you.'

Brook is listening, hanging on every word.

'Then you picked up on that, when I finally got home that night. You started telling me about your friend's abortion. You even told me you understood about handing over babies. And that changed things, love. That's what changed for us.'

'Yeah. It did. But how about Jonah? Nothing needed to change for him. He was always such a goody goody.'

'That's true. But you know, that can be a trap too.'

Carol smiles as she remembers the little boy who thought he was so big.

'He was so young, just a kid, when your dad left, but he thought he had to run the place. He took on being the good guy. He never let himself be trouble. And that's not such a healthy pattern either. Safe, but not so healthy. You were different. You were the explorer who took off by her little self. You felt safe enough to test all the boundaries.'

'Is that how you were?'

'Yes. Sort of. I got into some pretty bad habits. I'm glad I didn't have to parent me.'

'We didn't do much with your family, did we Mum? We didn't go to Sydney much like for big Christmas dinners with all the aunts and uncles and other kids. I often wondered why that was, especially when I saw my friends with their grandparents and cousins.'

'True. Part of it was we were scattered all over the place, north east and south west of the state, and then of course, Andrew in north America.'

Carol knows she hasn't answered Brook's real question, and she also knows it was true that after they all left home, her parents seemed to revert to being just a couple again. The chickens had fled. The coop door was shut tight.

'I guess we just do scattered families,' Brook said.

'Hey, Knock. Knock,' Carol says with a serious face.

Brook looks at her and answers 'Who's there?'

'Me. I'm there.'

Carol stretches out her arms wide, and Brook cuddles in.

'It still works, after all this time,' Carol says to herself.

They make hot cocoa and head off to bed.

※ ※ ※

Thoughts are swirling around Carol's head in the pitch dark silent room.

Scattered. She does not want to be scattered. She does not want to have bits of herself all over the place. She wants a home. She tries imagining herself in Sydney, in Jack's place. Mmmm. But her brain won't stay there.

She makes a list in her head. She ticks off Andrew as going as well as could be expected. With Jennifer, Carol makes a note to try harder. She ticks off her children. She ticks off her dad. There is Robert without a tick.

Finally Carol gets up and makes herself some notes. Phone Robert and do a detour to see him tomorrow. Phone work and to say she will be a day late. Phone Jack and make definite arrangements for Sydney next weekend. Phone Jennifer and see how she is going.

And yes, she reminds herself about gratitude. She gives thanks for her girl and the woman she has become, and she gives thanks for her boy who she thinks will always be OK. And she gives thanks for her dad and that she had the chance to get to know him and through him, her mum. And most of all she gives thanks for Jack. She reminds herself that it's OK, it's more than OK, to be wanted.

TWENTY ONE

First thing next morning Carol phones the local police to check the flood situation. It seems OK to drive through, for the present.

Another long morning in the car and she is at Robert's. He is standing waiting in front of his house with a big smile of welcome on his face. They touch. They gingerly move in for a long hug. She mounts the three wooden steps and finds a space in the mess on the verandah.

Robert too is messy. His hair has reverted to dreadlocks. His clothes look like he sleeps in them. His big frame is quite shrunken now. His chest caves in and he stoops, with his shoulder blades sticking out at the back.

But his steel blue eyes are bright. He meets her gaze. He keeps apologizing about the state of the house, till she tells him she has come to see him, not to do a house inspection. They both laugh about that.

She is reluctant to talk with him on the verandah. She needs to move after the long drive, and suggests he shows her the garden in this rented place. The garden is far from messy.

They put on gum boots and raincoats and walk, with Carol asking garden questions, and him answering.

Robert tells her the owner of the place has given him a monthly budget at the local nursery. He says that the owner values Robert's improvements, as he wants to move in himself one day.

The few hectares, once part of a horse stud of cleared land, are now a work in serious progress, with a bank of native trees on the southern boundary, forming a wind break from the severe winter weather. Vegetables grow in and around the fruit and nut trees. A winding drive to the house is edged with native shrubs so that his house is now hardly visible from the front gate. The open machinery shed houses an ancient ride-on mower that needs lots of encouragement and tender loving care. Robert reckons its days are numbered as he is experimenting with flowers and herbs to replace the grass and clover mix that make up the lawn.

'I'll always live on a place like this that has its own spring,' he says waving his arms around. 'This would have been impossible if you relied on the rain.'

She tells him he is doing such a wonderful job on this piece of land and he says this is what he does.

'You take a piece of land that has been neglected or misused,' he says, 'and you make it better, for the next person. It's like having children. Like our parents made it better for us, and you, with Jonah and Brook, you've made it better for them.'

'I'd never thought about it like that.' She wants to stow it away to think more about it later. There's a message there, in what Robert is saying.

'What you are doing with the land and what we are doing with children,' she says, 'it's micro. It's small scale. We're not doing so well on the macro.'

It's such a quiet 'No' from Robert she does not dare to follow up on the poisoned climate chalice they are leaving for their children and their children. So she points to the mound of mulch on the corner of the verandah. 'What's that?'

'That? Oh that's the remains of the brush turkey's nest. I promised him I would keep it there for next year.'

She admires his rambling vegetable garden.

'Yeah,' he says, 'well I don't get to the shops all that often so it's good to grow as much as I can here.'

They are both avoiding the hard stuff like 'How are you feeling?' 'How has it been lately?' He breaks the pattern with, 'Dad tells me you have a new bloke. I remember those Turner boys. They were fun.'

And suddenly she is doing all the talking. And Robert is her big brother again. And she's telling him all the good things about Jack, how he is kind and considerate and his own person and hasn't got any ties like kids or step-kids, and how he loves contact with all his brothers and all of his nieces and nephews. And she's telling him how Jack listens carefully when she raves on about all the family stuff, and how he wants her to start having weekends in his place in Sydney so that whenever she's ready she can move in full time. And she is telling him that she is ready for a big change, a move to Sydney, a different work scene but somehow scared about moving in with him.'

She stops for breath and asks, 'What do you think about me going into a serious relationship after this long time without a special man in my life?'

Robert says he needs to think about this for a few minutes.

Carol doesn't want to think about this for a few minutes. She fidgets.

But then Robert starts questioning her. Like does she really know him well enough and surely there are some downsides. And before she knows it she is telling him about Jack's 'thing' about climate change but it is more than a mind 'thing', it is so deep that it tips him into a rather scary space, and Robert, should she be worried about that?

Robert says she has come to the right place to talk about scary spaces.

And after that they both fall silent. For another whole round of the garden.

They go back to the house, and Robert fills the kettle and sets out the tea things on a dirty tray, and they take it all out to the verandah and sit on the floor among the dead leaves and twigs, which gives her plenty to pick at with her fingers.

'I know scary places,' he says. 'Scary places happen when they control you instead of you controlling them. Scary places are inhabited with things and people you cannot shut up. Even if you yell and scream into the empty paddocks, when you stop for breath, they are still there, in your head. The you shrinks. They grow. They gain possession. Yes.'

She waits while he gazes out to the garden gathering his thoughts.

'Then there are scary places that are real. Like wars. Like jumping off high cliffs. And some people put themselves in those places willingly, even proudly. And they don't call them mad, well the shrinks don't.'

He pauses again, and she wonders about the medication he has to take everyday of his life, and she feels so sad for him when she thinks how his mind used to dart around, taking everything in at once and how he could talk at top speed about anything and everything.

'And then there's the stuff you're talking about, little Sis. And some of us humans have a deeper knowing about the changes, not just with climate, but with disappearing species, and with fertile land that turns salty, and with exponential growth of the human population on a planet that isn't growing at all, and I don't think we can call that mad because it is all really happening, and even worse it will get worse when there is not enough fresh water, or fertile land or seafood. We don't even have a name for this scary human condition, and we don't have pills like I take, and we don't have a brand of counseling or therapy to deal with it. It is scary. It's seems like you've got yourself one of those people. And it seems that you are a bit scared about that.'

He looks at her with his big brother special eyes.

She nods.

Robert holds both of her hands. 'Tell yourself he is not mad. Tell yourself this is his thing, but this is not your thing. You, my little sister, are like an engineer for humans. You fix things. You get people to trust you and then you fix up their bodies. You cannot fix him. Right? Say it. You cannot fix him.'

She nods.

'Say it.'

'I cannot fix him.'

'So do you still want him?'

'Yes.'

'Good. He's a lucky guy. And little sister, you cannot fix me.'

She ignores the tears that have started to drip down her face.

'Carol, I am mad. Not all the time. Just some of the time. It's my life. Not yours. I love to see you, because you are so special to me, but I'm not part of the inheritance. I don't become yours when Dad dies, OK?'

'OK.'

He walks away around the corner of the verandah, and comes back to present her with a generous bouquet of fresh spinach leaves and an old bucket of mixed citrus fruit. Hug. And she head off south, in a car of delicious smells.

ACKNOWLEDGEMENTS

A big thank you to Evan Shapiro from Cilento Publishing who magically transforms a manuscript into a book. To my nit-pickers, my sister Leone Sperling and friend Suzanne Marks who drilled down on the punctuation, grammar and repetition. To Laurel Cohn whose professional wisdom and insight gave me gentle but direct guidance, and to my partner in life Hans Heilpern who had to share me with that other family that kept growing and taking over my head space.

Also by Sandra Heilpern

The Volvox

1. GONE

It is one week since Bella has gone. One week since that Tuesday when she disappeared from my life.

Bella was sixteen years, one month and two days when she set off for school that morning, that day, which neatly slices my life into two distinct parts – the time with Bella and the time since she has gone missing.

That morning did not seem to be any different to any other morning at our place. And I should know. I have lived it over and over in my mind almost every day since. I do replays. I change the script. I write myself in as a superbly vigilant mother, who notices and notes every little nuance, every word, every expression that Bella puts out. I even notice what she is not saying. I look across to the kitchen doorway, the moment she appears. I do eye contact. I look searchingly and concernedly into her face and ask her what she would like for breakfast. "Oh", I answer in surprise, "toast and vegemite," even though it has been toast and vegemite for the past thirteen years. I ask about her needs for the day. Does she need her sports clothes ironed? Would she like a packed lunch?

Who am I kidding? She would have shrugged me off with a "Oh Mum, do you have to?" and slumped down at the kitchen table putting her own slices of bread into the toaster, and warming her hands in the air above them as they cooked, as she did every single morning.

No. That morning was no different. Or, at least no different to me. While Bella's morning vegemite toast habit and her disdain for packed lunches gave some consistency to our lives, every day of living with Bella was a new experience. She was child. She was woman. She was manic energy, sloth, dancer, phone addict, insomniac, guitar strummer, high achiever, low achiever.

At sixteen. Bella turned adolescence into an art form.

And I lost her.

That day I lost her, I came home form work at the usual time, about a quarter to six. It was still light. I always rush home from work. I drive my car into the city and I pay exorbitant parking rates so that I can start my journey home to Bella the minute I finish work. No drinks after work. No hanging about for a gossip, or as we say in the public relations section, for a debrief. No staying late to impress the boss about my high levels of commitment. No. I put my head down and get on with it. I fit my overtime into an intense nine to five.

As soon after five as I can manage it, I throw my diary and a few files into my brief case, grab my car keys and dash to the lift, tapping my foot as the rows of red lights show me all the lifts which are above the twelfth floor or below it. I grimace as the lift mindlessly repeats its electronic message about having a nice day and when I am released, I click, click, click in my leather work shoes over the wide expanse of granite flooring and out the glass double doors. I dash across six lanes of crawling traffic to the underground car park and curve my way back up to the road. Shamelessly I dredge up all my aggressive driving tricks as I duck between lanes. The five pm news fades out on the car radio with the All Ordinaries Index and the overseas exchange rates on the Australian dollar. I have given up telling the radio this is useless information. It takes no notice.

The current affairs program entertains the listening part of my mind, while the automatic part clicks into its compulsive behaviour of counting traffic lights. Some other corner of my brain does the driving and the rest checks whether I need to shop on the way home. My single mother, working mother guilt does not let me stop for anything but the bare essentials, whatever they are. This guilt has laid low all day, but now it kicks in double time, with the thought of Bella, already home from school and by herself for at least an hour, except, of course, when she has after school sport, or music, or drops in to a friend's house on the way home.

My work friends give me such a bad time about rushing home to Bella. No, I tell them, time and time again, I can't do meetings at 5.30, I have to get home. I have a child. I'm a single Mum, you know. You lot wouldn't understand. Just wait until you have kids. OK, so she's a teenager. But look, she's home all by herself. I would mutter my explanations which were no explanation to them.

Twitters. Exchanges of knowing looks.

My morning fantasy of good mother pops up at various times during a bad day. Here I am, pulling the tray of biscuits out of the oven as Bella comes skipping through the open door of the house. The mother, who is there to listen about her day at school, who has tidied up the house and brought the clothes in from the line while they still smell of the sun and aren't the slightest bit damp.

But I can't do that image very often. Being that kind of mother would drive me crazy. It did drive me crazy as soon as Bella started pre-school so that I had to find my self respect and dust it off and fight my way back to work.

It would drive Bella crazy too. She doesn't want me picking up after her, hanging about for the perfect moment to catch her between her phone calls.

So why do I rush home? Well I guess it's my need, not Bella's, especially in the winter. I hate getting home after dark. Dark is when it should all be done by. Front door shut and dinner on the table. When I think about it, with honesty, this manic drive through the afternoon peak traffic is no different from the way I run the rest of my life. I want to be home, but not home all day. I want a real relationship with a man, but I don't want to live with one. Not yet. I want to keep seeing Geoff but I feel dreadful about his wife and kids. I want to work but I don't want to be doing the same old thing day after day. I want to save up for a holiday but I can't say no to most of what Bella asks for, or for what I ask for, for that matter. I want to be thin and I want to eat. I want to be fit and I just want to lie around most of the weekend. I don't want to give myself such a hard time but why is my life so fucking difficult?

But that day, exactly one week ago, I drove home from work as usual, and as soon as I put my key in the front door, I felt the emptiness of the house. Its emptiness entered my body, leaving a damp cold space. I shuddered as I took the shopping into the kitchen. I unlocked the back door and brought in the clothes, slightly damp as usual. I dumped the basket in the laundry. I went back into the kitchen and put on the kettle. I dragged myself upstairs and peeled off my work clothes and pulled on the sloppy tee shirt and tights from the chair next to my bed. I went back down into the kitchen, turned off the whistling kettle, made myself a pot of tea and sat down at the kitchen table.

I glanced over to the answering machine next to the phone. No blinking light. No messages. I sighed. Something was wrong. Something was very different. Something was missing. I knew nothing and I knew everything.

OK, I said to myself. OK Gina, just get it all together now. Turn on the radio. A bit of the old classical FM. That's better. Turn it up. Yeah. Fold laundry, take basket upstairs to the landing. Put away shopping. Put away breakfast dishes. Start dinner. Yeah.

I told myself I have until seven o'clock before I started worrying. But I was already worrying. Where was she? I checked the wall calendar again. I could hardly read it. There was so little room in each of those squares. There were arrows pointing to notes in the margins. There were notes scratched out and more notes written on top. Some of the writing was too small. I peered close trying to work it out. It was Wednesday 17th May. I could remember that much from work. The space in the 17 box was filled in with scribble – hers and mine. But, look, the "at Andrew's" was joined by a wavy line to "band practice" from the square before, and I remembered that she did go to Andrew's the day before, because she came home tired out from lugging her guitar case and said that next time she might just do flute instead. And there was something else written there. But it was only my writing and it was a note to remind me to confirm my air tickets if I wanted to go away with Geoff for the weekend that Bella was due to spend with her father next month, but I had scratched out that note myself, because, well, it doesn't really matter why. Except that deep down I knew that Geoff needed to sort things out one way or another with Anna before I can really go away with him and enjoy it..

So it was empty. That day's box had nothing in it after all. OK, I told myself. We both stuff up. Bell and me. Sometimes she forgets to put things up on the calendar, and sometimes I forget too. But I did not convince myself. Not at all.

Fear. Remember fear? Yes I remembered that lump of lead that plummets down, down to the pit of my stomach? I remembered the damp crawling over my skin. I remembered the smell of it on my body. I remembered it in Peter's eyes when I said that I had to get out. I remembered that fear, hanging in the air between our two astonished faces when he said, 'So go. So get out.'

I remembered that fear, and I recognised it that day. I raised my arm to my nose and I could smell it. I wanted to scream, 'No, this is too hard!'

I looked up Miranda's phone number. I made myself dial it. I talked to her Father. I gave the first warning, the first sign that all was far from well in our little household. The telephone conversation followed, almost to the word, the one that had been running in my head. No, Bella wasn't there. No, they hadn't seen her all afternoon. Yes, he'd just check with Miranda. No, Miranda hadn't seen her since school got out. No, Miranda hadn't caught the bus. Meredith had picked her up and they'd gone to the dentist. Look, Gina, perhaps I'd better come over. I can come straight away if you like.

I allowed myself one tiny pang of guilt about not having taken Bella to the dentist for over a year.

Yeah. Thanks. I guess I'm not really alright. Have your dinner first. But yeah, thanks, come by in about an hour and I'll do some more phoning around.

Looking back, that night was the worst. Miranda's dad, Guy, tried very hard to be helpful. We sat down and he started the lists. The first one was all the people Bella might have gone to see, gone out with, wanted to be with. The second list was all the people whom she might have said something to, about tonight, about not coming home. The third list was other contacts in her life, through music, through going on the same school bus, through staying over at her Dad's house, friends she hadn't seen for a while, friends of mine she got on well with. We became totally focussed on these lists. I hung these lists on the fridge, some with phone numbers, some with emails, some just names.

Guy said we should start on the first list. So, one by one, we phone them. One by one, we drew a blank but we didn't leave blanks. Oh no. We left Peter, my ex, hysterical and accusing. We left my brother Teff concerned and wanting to mount a full scale police inquiry.

We left trails of anguish with my friends, with the parents of Bella's friends, and when it was too late at night to worry any more people, we went around to the police. The young officer on duty, was polite enough, but he said we shouldn't take it too seriously if she didn't come home that night. He said we would be surprised how many teenagers stay away one or even a few nights, leaving their parents in a panic. To the police, missing wasn't missing until it was at least forty eight hours old. He said I should keep making lists.

I didn't sleep at all that night. By morning I had pages full of lists with as many contact details as I could find in my phone, my address book, my email lists, my head.

I needed to go to work. I took a photo of Bella with me. I scanned it into my computer. I worked it into a poster. Shamelessly I printed off 100 copies, using expensive coloured paper. Over the next few evenings, I put them in shops, on walls, near our home, near her school, everywhere I could think of. I phoned back our friends and relatives on the 'A' list and emailed them a poster to put up, anywhere, everywhere.

Now, a week down the track, I vent all my frustration and grief on bothering the police. Every day before work and then again after work, I call in at the local police station. I demand to know what they have done. I demand to see the evidence of their actions to date. I want to know what they intend to do. When? How? And then what? They have lots of statistics to comfort me with, like how many teenagers are reported missing in NSW every day, like how many return home after one night, three nights, one week. I am sure they also have statistics on how many teenagers are abducted and raped and murdered, but they don't trot those out.

At last the police are beginning to take Bella's disappearance seriously although they still talk about her as having run away. At one level, I find the subtle changes in them reassuring, at another I find it terrifying. I have filled in a missing person's report. I have left some of the posters with the police. They are making suggestions, like I should try and think of reasons why Bella might have left home. Sometimes, when they are being patient with me, I want to stay there and watch while they do things to find her. But I know that as soon as I leave, they get on with their crises for the day. When they are condescending to me I want to smash their faces in. I am following up on one of the police's rare suggestions. I phone Telstra and ask for a print out of the phone numbers to my home over the past three months. I have a long altercation with someone called Charles, and ask to be put through to his manager, who is someone called Simone, and I explain to her once more that, yes, I know I get this information with my phone bill but I can't seem to find the last one and anyway I want the most recent three months and I want them now. Somehow I don't want to tell the Telstra people that the police suggested this because my darling Bella has gone missing because I so do not like Charles and Simone it is none of their business.

To my shame, instead, I just cry and blubber and repeat over and over I want them now. It works. Simone asks if I would like the information emailed immediately. I back down with an ingratiating thank you so much, Simone, thank you so much.

Apart from my twice daily visits to interrogate the police, I am detached. My body gets out of bed, showers, makes coffee, drives to work. It gets through the day, answers the phone, writes drafts, walks around the city at lunch time. My body eats takeaways as it plonks itself down in front of TV at night, watches whatever, listens to the incoming phone calls through the answering machine. I hear friends checking in to see if I'm alright. No, I scream to the machine, I am not alright. People with unfamiliar voices leave names I do not recognise, till I realise they are the parents of Bella's friends, her teachers, her music teacher. I hit the erase button. All gone.

Bella's father Peter has taken to dropping over after he's had dinner with his new family. I know he does not want to be here but he wants to be at home even less. So he wanders in about nine and fiddles with the remote of the television. My brother Teff has also taken to dropping in about the same time. He and Peter have always got on. I could never see what they had in common. Now they sit and chat a bit while Peter flips the channels. Teff does not go insane at this behaviour. He understands that this is what Peter needs to do. I get them cups of coffee and go up to bed, leaving them to let themselves out, whenever. I half hear their voices from the room below, and drift in and out of the lightest of sleep with the radio on for comfort. Anything but the silence. Silence is the window for thoughts that need to be shut out.

Silence brings images before my eyes whether they are shut or open. Silence makes me cry. I repeat the mantra that I must hold myself together, but I have no idea for what. I do not give in.

Except when I see Alma. Once a week I sit curled up in the big floppy arm chair facing Alma, my therapist. Last Friday, as I worked my way through the square box of tissues on the white cane table between us, Alma gently, and not so gently, led me out of numbness and into the terrifying world of feelings. Alma is very good at this. She leads and I follow. She and I have had months of practice.

Last night, when Peter and Teff were over, we printed off the Telstra email with all the phone numbers. I was amazed how much phoning in and out Bella and I can do in 12 weeks, well mostly Bella.

I got my lists from the fridge door and together we tried to match more phone numbers to names. It took hours. Teff had the most recent sheets and he picked up that there were phone ins from public phone boxes. They certainly weren't my calls. I promised I would take this to the police in the morning.

My rational mind keeps telling me that Bella is not dead. I know that there are thousand of run-away teenagers in this city. I know that, whatever her reasons are, Bella is not running away from anything. I know that there is nothing in her life that is so horrible, so scary that it is making her run away. If she has run, then she must be running away to someone, to do something, for some reason that I don't know about. My rational mind is little comfort to me now. It can reason away as long as it likes, I am scared.

The hardest thing is not knowing where she is. The second hardest thing is not knowing why she has run away. And the third hardest thing is the fear I detect in other people – their fear that she is dead. I see it in their faces. I stay away from those people.

Alma is helping me look at the loss. Actually, Alma has been helping me deal with loss for almost a year now. Loss is something I seem to specialise in. I can count the main losses which make big holes inside me. The loss of my mother and the loss of the mother I would have much preferred. The loss of my father whom I hardly ever saw and who did not want to know me. The loss of childhood or the childhood that I wanted – with fun, and other kids running around the house, and two parents who were young and alive.

But now I need Alma to help me with losing Bella. The others have been dry runs for this loss. This is the big mother of all losses. I feel overwhelming shame that I have lost her. That I have been honoured with the gift of this extraordinary child and I don't deserve it. My shame is about not noticing the tell-tale signs. My shame is about being too busy or distracted with my own life to notice that she was in some sort of crisis. How can a mother live with her own child and not be 'there' enough for her?

And now she is somewhere else. Gone.

THE VOLVOX
is available for Kindle and POD at

www.cilentopublishing.com

AUTHOR BIOGRAPHY

Sandra Heilpern cares deeply about environmental and social justice issues. She does not consider herself a writer and only does so when she can no longer deny that 'something' just has to get out.

AUTHOR NOTE

If you enjoyed *Like There's no Tomorrow*, please consider writing a review and posting it on Amazon and other shop websites, Goodreads, or your own blog. As an independent author, I'm reliant on word-of-mouth recommendations and I would greatly appreciate your rating and/or review.

For more titles from Cilento Publishing go to
www.cilentopublishing.com

www.ingramcontent.com/pod-product-compliance
Lightning Source LLC
Chambersburg PA
CBHW060220180626
46813CB00007B/2893